SCAR CITY

JOEL LANE

SCAR CITY

Influx Press
London

Published by Influx Press
The Greenhouse
49 Green Lanes, London, N16 9BU
www.influxpress.com / @InfluxPress

This edition 2020.
Printed and bound in the UK by TJ Books.
First published in the UK in 2016 by Eibonvale Press.

Paperback ISBN: 9781910312612
Ebook ISBN: 9781910312629

Proofreader: Dan Coxon
Cover design: Vince Haig
Interior design: Vince Haig

CONTENTS

INTRODUCTION
NICHOLAS ROYLE

Scar City is Joel Lane's fifth collection of short fiction. Or his sixth, depending on whether you count *Do Not Pass Go*, a chapbook of crime stories published by Nine Arches Press in 2011, as a 'full' collection. That mini-collection is an important one in the make-up of *Scar City*, as we will see. I think I prefer to think of *Do Not Pass Go*, which included five stories, as a full collection, just a short one, but maybe it is helpful to distinguish in some way between a collection of five stories and one, such as *Scar City*, including twenty-two. I don't actually know how helpful.

I wish we could ask Joel Lane for his opinion, but we can't. The author died, unexpectedly, in November 2013, at the age of fifty. *Scar City* was published almost two years later, in October 2015, by David Rix's Eibonvale Press. Before he died, Lane had been hopeful that Eibonvale would publish the collection, but Rix had not confirmed his acceptance of the manuscript. In a note in the 2015 edition, Rix explained how he realised, when he heard about Lane's death, that in his drafts folder was an email to the author confirming he would publish it. For some reason, he had not yet sent it.

If these stories were published anonymously, Lane's fans would soon identify their author. All his recurrent motifs and images are here. Ash (or ashes), smoke, mist, fluid, vapour and, unsurprisingly, scars. Vulnerable individuals, characters who are hurting and who hurt others (sometimes the same characters do both). We feel sympathy for his characters, as he undoubtedly did, but their environments are pitiless – and not only the built ones. The climate bears down; even the seasons are brutal. 'As autumn hardened into winter,' we read in 'Echoland', 'their lives changed fast.' And you can bet it won't be for the better. In 'Feels Like Underground', a collaboration with another Birmingham-based author, Chris Morgan, we read, 'Winter felt like an absence, not a season at all.' The narrator of 'A Long Winter' is unusually forthright: 'The start of winter is always fucking miserable.' Nor should we think that Lee Winter, in 'Rituals', has a name just plucked from the air. (Although I wouldn't make the same claim for Donna Summer, name-checked in 'Feels Like Underground'.)

The one good thing about winter, in these stories, is that it doesn't last for ever. It's a relief to read, in 'Birds of Prey', that 'Winter brightened into spring.' But before we get complacent, 'Those Who Remember' reminds us that spring can hurt, too: 'The knife struck me again, but the tissues of my body were already corroding and flaking apart, the bones melting like ice in spring.' Still, there is always summer to look forward to. However: 'After a mild winter and a spring of feverish rain, the summer had a dull and stagnant feel' ('The Last Gallery'). Before you know it, 'The summer passed by like the heat from a distant fire' ('Making Babies'), and 'By then it was autumn, and a bitter wind was blowing in from the iron sea' ('The Grief of Seagulls').

Lane's characters have always faced a range of challenges. It's probably fair and not misleading to include among these the settings of his stories, which are often, but not always, districts of Birmingham and the West Midlands. Harsh though these urban landscapes may be, Lane's descriptions of them are among the chief pleasures of reading his work. Although he was born in Exeter and studied in Cambridge (where he achieved a first in History and Philosophy of Science), Lane spent most of his life in Birmingham, where he moved between Moseley, Acocks Green, Selly Oak, Handsworth and, at the end of his life, Tyseley. Acocks Green is described, in 'Making Babies', as 'a transition zone between the industrial estates of Tyseley and the yuppie theme park that was Solihull. These forces had warped the district from its placid suburban origins to a kind of tense emptiness, like the hollow inside a guitar.' For Lee, in 'Internal Colonies', 'There's probably enough Semtex stashed away in basements in Acocks Green to blow up the whole city.' Subtler, but perhaps more damning, is a throwaway remark in 'This Night Last Woman': 'By Acocks Green standards, it was quite a mixed crowd.'

Mark, in 'Among the Leaves', lives in Shard End, 'a long bus ride out through council estates that were like a child's construction kit, most of the pieces having been trodden on or lost. Flat shopping arcades, encased in shells of concrete, were coiled around pale and glassy-eyed tower blocks. Small fragments of routine life were visible amongst the marks of violence and neglect: a window box, clothes on a washing line, the cocked ear of a satellite dish. In many buildings, the only occupants were squatters.' Shard End, when we eventually get there, is 'slightly more reassuring: terraced houses painted in various colours; trees whose heads were turning to gold; a primary school so heavily armoured it might have been a military barracks.' Only slightly, then.

A couple of miles south of Shard End you'll find Yardley. In 'By Night He Could Not See', Yardley's Swan Centre has been demolished. 'The knot of reeking subways in front of it had been replaced by a concrete walkway over the Coventry Road that trembled from all the cars passing through. Yardley felt more like an airport than a district now. You couldn't stand still without getting vertigo.' Lane was a Gregory Award-winning poet as well as a short story writer, novelist, essayist and anthologist; that couplet, the pair of sentences at the end of the Yardley quote, remind us of this.

As for Tyseley, where Lane lived in a flat on the Warwick Road, it is referenced on a few occasions, none more telling than in an exchange of dialogue in 'This Night Last Woman'. One character asks another, '"How's life here?"' (I'm deliberately not saying where 'here' is.) The answer comes, '"Not so bad. When you've lived in Tyseley, it all becomes relative."'

Digbeth has featured in Lane's work throughout his career, rarely in a positive light. Here it is home to 'Victorian urinals and long-abandoned cars' ('Rituals') and, in 'The Last Gallery', the district is 'trapped in a state of transition: old buildings half-demolished, new buildings half-finished'. But it also appears to offer a possible entry point to the mythical cityscape of Echoland in the story of that name: 'Certain places felt close to it: the old viaduct in Digbeth, where narrow roads passed under the black arches…' Echoland, 'a vision all humanity could share', recalls Vitraea, the fabled land that might be glimpsed at the bottom of a bottle in Lane's story 'The Country of Glass', originally published in *Dark Terrors 4*, edited by Stephen Jones and David Sutton, and reprinted in Lane's 2006 collection *The Lost District*, which in turn had surely drawn inspiration from M. John Harrison's short story 'Egnaro'.

Other backdrops are available – Macclesfield, Croydon, Fishguard, Aberdeen, Milton Keynes ('a town that had been designed by cars') and another equally fantastical location, Carcosa, borrowed from Ambrose Bierce via Robert W. Chambers (and Joseph S. Pulver, Sr., who edited *A Season in Carcosa*, in which Lane's story 'My Voice is Dead' first appeared) – but most of the time we are in the West Midlands.

Sometimes I think that if my life were to fall apart, I might move to Birmingham and spend the rest of my days walking around its outlying districts reading Joel's stories. I don't mean to suggest that the West Midlands should be a destination to consider only when all else has failed; rather it's an option, a positive choice, a source of comfort. I'd probably steer clear of the Acocks Green pub in 'This Night Last Woman', despite its being one of the best stories in this collection, with a great red herring and a brilliant payoff and another one of those couplets, like in 'By Night He Could Not See', that show, at micro level, what a superb craftsman Lane was: 'Her face was a mask. It felt like I'd known her all my life.'

He was also very funny, both on the page and in company. I remember him giving a reading at a convention of a pastiche he had written – something about a man with sausages for fingers. A packed room was in stitches; he had that crowd in the palm of his sausage-fingered hand. There's a story in *Scar City* that turns on a pun, and in 'Feels Like Underground' there's a joke about time management that made me laugh out loud.

I realised, when reading the collection in preparation for writing this introduction, that I had not actually read it when it came out. I had read lots of the stories before, but I hadn't read them together, and there were several I had never read at all. It was a surprise to me that I hadn't previously sat down – or walked around – and read it and I wondered why. The book was printed by Lightning Source and I don't like reading books printed by Lightning Source. They don't look right, they don't feel right. Sometimes you turn the page and you find you've turned two pages at once. But my objection to Lightning Source books wouldn't have been a good enough reason not to read this posthumous collection. And there's the answer. It would have been the extreme poignancy of the thought of David Rix's unsent email – the pain it had caused Rix and the pain it would cause me to think about it, both for Rix's sake and for Lane's, since Joel and I had been close friends for many years.

In his note Rix also wrote that he had been unable to find any record of previous publication for three of the stories – 'Internal Colonies', 'A Long Winter' and 'Rituals'. In fact, one of these, 'Rituals', had been included in *Do Not Pass Go*, along with 'This Night Last Woman', and if Rix should have spotted that, so should I have done when he asked me for help. As for the other two, my guess is they were intended as original publications. Lane was a pro and had published four – or five – previous collections; he knew that the convention was to include two or three original stories among the reprints.

I sometimes open that Eibonvale Press edition of *Scar City* looking for Joel's handwritten dedication. Most of my copies of his books have generous and often funny little dedications in his distinctive tiny handwriting, a blue ballpoint pressed hard on the page or a black Pentel Rollerball, but not this one. Obviously. I say 'obviously', but I forget, partly because when you're reading the stories, it's like he hasn't gone anywhere. He's still there. Still at the karaoke night in Acocks Green, still navigating the narrow Digbeth backstreets, still wandering past those Moseley pubs and walking up and down the Warwick Road in Tyseley.

THOSE WHO REMEMBER

Night had fallen when I reached Oldbury. The best time for coming home: when the new developments fade into the background and the past becomes real again. Over the years I'd seen expressways carve up the landscape and titanic, jerry-built tower blocks loom above the familiar terraces. The town was boxed in by industrial estates built on the sites of old factories. Instead of real things like steel and brick, the new businesses manufactured 'office space' and 'electronics'. Only the night could make me feel at home. The night and seeing Dean again.

He took some finding this time. The windows of his old house were boarded up, and two short planks had been nailed across the front door: one at the top, one at the bottom. If they'd been nailed together, I could believe it was still his home. It was hard to imagine him leaving the area, but maybe he was dead or in prison.

I walked around the streets for hours. Everything had changed except the people. The teenagers had designer tops and mobile phones now, but they fought in car parks and fucked in alleys just as they had when I was a teenager. Local industry was dying then; it was dead now. Opposite a new multi-storey car park, I saw the old cinema where Dean and I had gone to see *Butch Cassidy and the Sundance Kid* when we were twelve. The doorway and windows were bricked up.

The next morning, I checked the phone book. Dean was living in one of the tower blocks north of the town centre. Where the council stuck people who had, or were, problems. It saved the social services a lot of petrol. I could see the towers from my hostel room: three grey rectangles cut out of the white sky. Gulls flying around them like flakes of ash, probably drawn by the heaps of rubbish on the slope.

I walked through the town, past the drive-in McDonald's that was now its chief landmark. A narrow estate, with tiny cube-shaped flats in rows three or four deep, seemed to be in the process of demolition: half of the cubes were broken up, their blank interiors exposed to the weak morning light. It had been much the same three years earlier. I try to come back every now and then, without letting Dean know my plans. I prefer to surprise him. At least the wasteground with the remains of a derelict house, where he and his mates Wayne and Richard had beaten me senseless in 1979, was still here. I walked through it, glancing around for the teeth I'd lost. One day they'd turn up.

Climbing the bare hill to the three towers, I passed a few children who were stoning an old van. They'd taken out most of the windscreen. I waited at the entrance to the second tower until a young woman dressed in black came out; I slipped in past her. It seemed colder inside the building than outside; the stone steps reeked of piss and cleaning fluids. Dean's flat was on the ninth floor. While climbing, I rehearsed what I was going to make him do.

After ten minutes of ringing, the door finally opened. He was looking rough, less than half awake. The kind of piecemeal shave that's worse than none at all. Shadows like old bruises round his eyes, which were flecked with blood. 'What are you after?' he said. 'I don't feel too good. Come back later.'

'Not a chance.' I took his shaky hand off the door and pushed it further open, then walked in. The smell of despair washed over me: three parts sweat, two parts stale food and booze, one part something like burnt plastic. The curtains were shut. I raised a hand. 'Miss Havisham, I have returned – to let in the light!'

Dean laughed. 'Gary, have you seen the view?' He probably had a point. I shifted a few dusty magazines to make space on the couch, then sat down. 'It's been a long time,' he said. 'Why have you come back? I don't need you.'

'Yeah, you're doing just fine on your own.' I looked around his living room. Boxes and suitcases were stacked against the far wall, under a stain like a deformed spider. 'Have you just moved in, or are you leaving?'

It took him a while to get the point. 'Been here a couple of years,' he said. 'Lost my job, tried to sell the house but it needed too much work. Council found me this flat. It'll do while I get myself sorted out.'

'Sure.' The burnt plastic smell was troubling me. 'Have you had a short circuit or something? Cable burning out?'

Again, he had to think for a bit. 'I was cooking up some breakfast.'

'Excellent. Haven't had a bacon butty in ages.'

'Oh, I've put it all away now. In case…' His eyes closed.

I stood up wearily and walked over to him, looked closely at his face. His eyes opened again; he looked away. 'Dean, there were three things you could never keep. A promise, a bank account and a secret. What is it this time?'

'Nothing.' He put a hand to his mouth, then staggered. 'Fuck.'

'I'd rather have a coffee to start with.'

Dean gave me a look of utter contempt, then staggered through a side door. I could hear him throwing up in the toilet. The magazines on the couch were his usual blend of soft porn, war and the paranormal. He came back after a minute, looking sweaty. 'Need to go out for a while,' he said.

'Sit down first. I want to talk to you.' He shrugged and balanced his lean arse on a plastic chair. 'Have you done any work since you moved here?'

'Building… sometimes. More demo than building. It's all casual now, you take what you can get.' I remembered he'd started a one-man repair firm in his twenties. Hadn't lasted long. He'd kept a horse tethered to his gate.

'What about Richard and Wayne? Do you still work for them?'

I saw a flicker of recognition in his eyes. Maybe he was starting to remember. 'I never worked for them,' he said. 'Just the odd bit of business. You know?' I nodded. 'Look, I need to go out now. Got a job interview.'

He was wearing a torn grey fabric top, stained jeans and trainers without laces. They might have had a certain urchin appeal if he'd been sixteen instead of forty-one. But he'd always been sixteen to me, so it didn't matter. An employer might feel differently.

I reached out, gripped his hand. It felt cold and thin. I pulled his sleeve back to the elbow and saw the tracks. He didn't try to stop me. He was drifting off again. 'Dean, I'm going to help you,' I said. 'And that means you're not going anywhere for a while. Tough love. We'll get through this together. And afterwards, I need you to help me.'

Dean leaned forward and held onto the wall. A thin stream of drool ran from the corner of his mouth. Then, suddenly, he ran for the door. I stopped him. 'Fuck off, fuck off, fuck off,' he kept repeating. I held him until he curled up on the floor, his hands over his head, and went to sleep.

The next three days were hard work. I took Dean's keys and kept the flat locked. He wasn't that likely to jump out the window from the ninth floor. A search of his bedroom revealed a battered set of works, a couple of syringes and a plastic bag with a few meagre traces of powder. I destroyed all of it. While he was asleep I slipped out to buy bread, milk and bleach, then cleaned the flat as best I could. While he was awake I listened to his rantings, his promises and threats, his explanations and frantic pleas. I cleaned him when he shat and threw up over himself. I wiped the sickly, malodorous sweat from his face and body. And yes, I gave him a couple of handjobs when he became aroused. I have to take some gratification where I can find it. Though I got rather more pleasure from throwing his mobile phone out the window, not even hearing it strike the gravel far below.

After three days, I decided he'd got through the 'cold turkey' process and was ready for the next stage. Of course, he'd only keep off the smack with ongoing support to help him fight the craving. But to be honest, that wasn't my concern. He was always in trouble: the last time it had been diazepam, and a couple of times before that he'd been drinking himself blind. I always did what I could to clean him up, put him back on the path. But he'd never had much sense. Like some historian said, those who forget the past are condemned to repeat it.

And those who remember do it anyway.

When I gave Dean back his keys, he was a different man. His clothes were washed and he'd had a healthy breakfast. His flat was still a dump, but it was a cleaner dump that smelt only of pine-scented bleach. He smiled at me, and I could almost have kissed him. 'Now I need you to do something for me,' I said. He waited. 'First we're going out for a decent coffee. Then I want you to find Wayne and Richard. And help me kill them.'

Dean made the call from an infected phone box on the estate of broken cubes. Said he was clean but had debts to pay. He wasn't kidding. Richard said Wayne was away cutting some overgrown grass. He'd be back tomorrow. They could meet in the usual place. That was the derelict house, Dean explained to me; or rather what was left of it. I was touched to realise I wasn't the only person trapped in the past. The death of religion has left us all to create our own rituals.

We walked out past the Homebase to the new junction, a twisted structure gleaming with light. The gateway to the future. Cars streamed above us as I explained to Dean what he was going to do. 'It's not just what they did to me,' I said. 'You'll never have a decent life while they're around. They know far too much about you. That's why you can't leave this shithole. It has to end. Ten seconds and we'll both be free. Then I'll leave you alone.'

He stared at me in a confused way. The years of alcohol and drugs had taken their toll. And he'd hardly been the brightest light on the tree to begin with. 'There's no other way,' I said, and handed him the knife. He touched his finger to the blade, licked the blood off his fingertip. Then he turned the knife over and over in his hands, gazing at it. I think he knew where it had come from, but I moved us on before he could think too much.

'I need money for a new mobile,' he said as we walked back through the town. I had no idea what they cost, but took fifty quid from my old wallet and handed it to him. We passed a branch of Dixon's, but he didn't stop. He was trembling. For a moment I could see him as a teenager, walking up that mountainside in North Wales.

As we neared the estate, I asked him: 'What about that mobile?'

'I need a date first,' he said without looking at me. 'Now I'm off drugs, I've got the urge back. There's a girl on the fourteenth floor of my block. She'll do everything for fifty. Tomorrow could go wrong, Gary. I deserve it.'

'You always were the romantic type.' I briefly considered just pushing his face through a window. But that wouldn't be enough. 'I'll leave you to it, Romeo. Be outside your block tomorrow morning at twelve. Or fucking else.'

The town streets were jammed with traffic, workers on their lunch break, pensioners hunting for cheap food. The

7

air was getting warmer, but I was too cold inside to derive much comfort from that. I bought a four-pack of Diamond White, took it back to my hostel room and drank off all the bottles without a break. Thinking about the derelict house: four shattered walls, a few heaps of timber, flakes of plaster, exposed wires. Then I thought of some tents on a hillside in Wales, stars glittering in the open sky like flaws in ice. Finally I drew the curtains, lay down and pretended to sleep. That was the only way I could make myself think of nothing.

———

'I'm not doing it.' He was wearing a battered leather jacket, but still shivering. The sky behind the three tower blocks was the grey of dead skin. He cupped his thin hands and blew into them, shaking his head.

'Are you back on the fucking horse?'

'No, I told you, a date. She fucking loved it.'

'Spare me,' I said. 'The most romantic thing a girl's ever said to you is *Is it in yet?*'

Dean gazed down the hill at the shattered boxes where people had lived. Where they maybe still did. 'They're my mates,' he said. 'What do you know about friendship?'

'I know a gayboy when I see one.'

'Why, you look in the mirror? I like women.'

'Gail didn't love it, did she?'

He looked at me then, confusion and panic in his face. 'What are you talking about?'

'I'm talking about the one chance you've got to show you're a man. A human being of any kind. Those two don't deserve to walk the streets, and you know it. Or are you just going to spend the rest of your useless life in that derelict house, the two of them taking turns to come in your mouth?'

He started walking down the hill towards the estate. 'Don't need a fucking syringe, do I? You never give up jabbing the needle in.'

At the edge of the wasteground, he stopped again. 'Can't see them. They're going to jump on us.'

'You wish.' I was losing patience. 'I'm with you, remember. It's two against two. I know you prefer three against one. But we've got the advantage. Let's get this over with, for fuck's sake.' I shoved him forward. 'Loser. Coward. Fairy. Don't you know what the knife is for? You used to.'

He walked on fast over the wet, uneven ground. The remains of the derelict house were on the far side: a blackened structure only four or five feet high, with part of an empty window frame in one broken wall. The doorway had long since collapsed, and you had to climb over the crumbling bricks to get through. There was no longer any roof. Two figures were waiting on either side of the few mouldering stairs. They'd put on some weight.

'Who's this fucker?' I wasn't sure if it was Wayne or Richard speaking.

'I think you know,' Dean said quietly. 'He's been here before.'

'You're fucking kidding,' the other one said. Dean whipped the knife out of his coat pocket, gave a wordless cry, and charged at him.

Richard, I think it was, kicked him hard in the stomach. Wayne grabbed his right arm and snapped the wrist with a single carefully aimed karate chop. The knife dropped soundlessly onto the rotting stairs. Dean fell to his knees and vomited. I stood outside the ruin, watching through the empty window frame.

The two men worked him over for a couple of minutes, doing no serious damage, but inflicting as much pain as they could. They left him lying on his back, twitching and drooling blood. As an afterthought, Wayne pissed over him. Then they walked out without glancing in my direction. They walked away fast, as if they had other business to attend to.

It took Dean an hour to regain consciousness. Bruising had closed his left eye, and blood had crusted over his mouth. He looked like a poorly made-up circus clown. He lifted his right arm and moaned with pain. Then he saw me standing inside the half-wall, watching him. All his memories were coming back. 'What's wrong?' I asked. 'Don't you like it that way?'

His damaged mouth tried to say something, but I couldn't tell what. 'Why don't you finish it?' I said. 'I'll let you off the fuck this time. They beat you up too much. Just use the knife.' I picked it up and wiped the flecks of plaster from the handle, then put it in his left hand. Dean struggled to his knees. I slipped off my jacket, turned my back to him and put my hands on the window frame.

The knife went in between my ribs, just to the right of the spine. It was more a carving than a stabbing action. My back arched in the ecstasy of release. I saw my last breath like a scar on the petrol-tinged air. The knife struck me again, but the tissues of my body were already corroding and flaking apart, the bones melting like ice in spring. By the time he let go of the knife and began his long, painful walk to the town, there was nothing left of me.

Dean was the only one of the three who went on the camping trip to Wales where we climbed a mountain and put up cheap tents in a sloping field. I shared a tent with a boy called Alan. In the night some of the boys visited the girls' tents. I just lay there, pretending to sleep.

Long after midnight, someone crept in through the tent-flap. It wasn't Alan, who'd gone out an hour before: it was Dean. He told me Gail, the red-haired girl, had refused him. 'I'm not good enough for her. So I thought, I know who I'm good enough for.'

He fucked me slowly, without spit or tenderness. Afterwards he lay there as if stunned. I asked: 'Aren't you going to finish me off?'

He laughed as if I'd made a joke, then grabbed my arm. 'Come with me.' We got dressed and left the tent. I'd never seen night outside the city before, couldn't believe how bright the stars were. Dean led me to a footpath that curved away from the field into a wooded area that reached up the mountainside. It was midsummer, but I felt cold. His sperm was trickling into my underpants. I no longer wanted any reciprocal contact. But I kept walking until the footpath led us out of the trees to a ridge overlooking a steep rock face and a tree-lined valley. 'Stop here,' he said.

I turned to face him. He was breathing heavily, and wouldn't meet my eyes. 'You want me to finish you off?' I didn't answer. 'Turn round.'

A terrible chill spread from between my shoulder blades through my whole body. The knife stayed in my back as I fell towards the dark trees. I was still alive when I hit the ground, and for hours afterwards. But nobody found me.

Nobody ever found me, or the knife.

That's another reunion done with. I'll be back next year, or the year after, or a couple of years after that. I like to surprise him. But the scene is decaying. Maybe next time they'll kill him. Or else he'll kill himself, with drugs or booze if not with violence. Nothing lasts forever, and there's no eternal. Everything falls apart in the end.

IN THIS BLUE SHADE

Lee was woken by a voice speaking into his ear. But when he raised his head to look around the dusty, curtained bedroom, the voice had gone. He must have dreamt it. Instead of drawing him deeper into the dream so he could answer, it had woken him up so he couldn't remember the question. That was people for you. Too rattled to lie in bed, he stumbled to the toilet and the shower. At least he wasn't hung over, though that probably meant he was still a bit drunk. And there was work to be done. No time for self-pity, or any other kind.

Snow had fallen overnight, but not very much. Like the icing on the cheap buns he remembered from childhood. Lee was sipping a mug of black Java coffee, feeling its caffeine filter through his system, when the post thudded onto the doormat. A pile of squarish white envelopes. Six cards, no bills: it was all good. He took them through into the kitchen, lit a cigarette and began to tear open the envelopes. At once, the familiar sight of thin furry creatures with sad eyes. Meercats: the most useless pop-culture icon since Flat Eric. More cards from business associates and distant relatives. Nothing from… who? Since his mother had passed away there wasn't anyone for him to miss getting a card from. He must have still been drunk.

The last card he opened showed a landscape: the sun setting behind a snowbound forest. It was a painting that mimicked a poorly focused photograph: the nearest tree had a low branch whose twigs were blurred, shimmering like a razor blade. The light through the trees was blue. But the sun was white with a dull yellow corona, and the trees were black. Only their shadows were blue. Lee thought he recognised the image. It was a painting that had hung on the front-room wall in his parents' house, but disappeared after they broke up. He'd asked them both about it, many years ago, but neither had known where it was. The card had no message, only his name and a formless signature that he thought was Ben's, an old boyfriend from his college days. They were still on good terms. It was the only non-meercat card of the batch.

After some toast and another cigarette, Lee shaved in the rusty bathroom mirror and put on his suit. He always tried to look good for the office: you never knew who'd turn up. There were only three working days left before Christmas, and a few loose ends to tie up. And once you'd got them tied up, there were important things to get out of them or knock into them. It was hard work. You had to think of consequences: set things up correctly, make sure nothing went wrong afterwards. It hadn't always been that way, but modern life was a disappointment. And around this time of year, there was always one you couldn't let go: one who ended up cold. He made sure of that.

It had been a long day. Six hours in the office, a hasty pub meal and an evening of paying visits with his team. Lee didn't much like outcalls: he preferred it when they came to him. If you had to drop in on them, it was more likely to turn nasty even if you hadn't planned it that way. And he didn't enjoy hurting people. It was just a means of persuasion. If he had to finish someone, he tried to avoid causing pain. Which meant, of course, that he could scare the living daylights out of certain people by being nice to them. You saw the relief when the first blow landed, though that didn't last long. His team were steadfast enemies of such complacency.

They didn't only hurt 'their own': a few rival operatives and even civilians earned it too. The last of tonight's targets was a case in point. A youth who'd been selling weed to his mates, undercutting the firm. They'd considered a warning, but he was a known bigmouth and termination was safer. The team had joined him in the pub when he was three sheets to the wind. Walked him out into the street, arms around his shoulders, all friends together, a gun touching his ribs. A short walk to the canal. No need to fire the gun. Kids with drug problems often drowned themselves, it was nobody's fault. Except maybe the parents.

Remnants of the snow had frozen on the path. Lee struggled with his front door, which the cold had warped out of true. I don't know how much more of this I can take.

That line was usually a comfort to him. But tonight it was literally hard to close the door, and that somehow made it harder to shut out certain thoughts in his mind as well. He poured himself a large Black Bush and lit a cigarette. A siren wailed; blue light flashed against the curtain. Lee tensed, but the pulsing light and sound faded. It was just past eleven. No work tomorrow. He needed some company.

How had things ended up like this? He'd always been a hard case, needed to be, but violence hadn't been his chosen career path. With his accountancy diploma he'd been a business manager for the firm, sorting out its financial affairs, keeping up the respectable front. He'd suggested a few changes to improve the firm's reputation. But given the calibre of local villains, it wasn't enough to make rules: you had to enforce them. And then there was Alan's death. He supposed the enforcer role had been a way of dealing with that. Five years later, he was still trying to deal with it.

He and Alan had met through the firm's business, got on well enough, and then met by chance in the Nightingale a few months later. They'd shared a few drinks and swapped phone numbers, and both men had gone home alone. Within a month they were dating steadily. Alan was a document forger, a specialist on the periphery of the firm. His hands were gentle and skilled. The relationship had started in January and ended in December the following year. They'd quarrelled about a few things near the end – Alan had met Charlie and was showing a different side to his nature, both aggressive and secretive. And inevitably, he was getting into debt. Lee was drinking more – partly to keep up with Alan's highs, partly to mask his own unhappiness. Someone in the firm had warned him that Alan was getting in too deep with certain people, there was going to be trouble. He'd meant to talk to Alan about it, but one glimpse of his lover's eyes had told him it was a waste of time. So he'd waited for Alan to learn whatever lesson was coming. Forgetting, somehow, that such lessons were usually written in blood.

Lee had never found out who'd snapped the forger's neck with a baseball bat and left him in the Sandwell Valley for rats to plunder. Nor why Alan had gone to the Valley, though two possible reasons came to mind. Sometimes he still wondered whether the firm was responsible. Taking on the enforcement – or punishment – role hadn't brought him any nearer to the answer. But it had proven his toughness, at least in the firm's eyes, and had given him an outlet for his anger. And after a few years, he'd gone on doing it for the reason most of us do things: it was what he did.

The glass was empty. He could go on drinking until he no longer cared, or he could do something to make the loneliness go away. What the fuck, it was Christmas. Lee picked up his black mobile and dialled the agency's number. They knew him, he didn't need to tell them what exactly he was looking for. An hour, the voice said. He rang off and drifted around the house, tidying things, smoking a cigarette, cleaning his teeth, making the bed, with 'Back In Black' playing low on the stereo in the living room.

The youth came to the door alone, wearing a hooded winter coat. A driver was sitting in a car parked across the road. Lee struggled with the door and asked the visitor to come in. Without his coat, Jason (almost certainly not his real name) looked rather like a meercat: a mop of hair above a slightly pouchy face and a thin body. He was twenty or so. Lee wasn't keen on boys as such – they always seemed to be mentally elsewhere – but young men could bring him back to a sense of being human.

Jason accepted a glass of wine and they made the usual small talk. He said he lived in Great Barr; Lee spared him the obvious pun. They sat on the black leather sofa and shared a cigarette. Blue fibres of smoke floated in the twilit room. Lee suggested they have a shower together.

They soaped each other gently as steam filled the bathroom. Lee kissed the youth, then turned off the water and dried them both with a white fluffy towel. This ritual always took him back to the changing rooms in school. The winter archive of loneliness. He spread the towel on the bathroom floor and asked Jason to stand on it. Then he knelt down and guided Jason's hands to the back of his head. It was like the question in his dream, but this time he knew the answer.

Later, as they were dressing, he said: 'I'd like to see you again. Can you do an incall this weekend? At your place, I mean?'

'It's not up to much, you know? I'd rather meet in a hotel room.'

Lee touched the youth's arm. 'Please, I'd like a date at your place. It's more exciting. I don't mind paying extra.'

Jason nodded. His hair fell into his face. 'Okay. Sort it out with the agency. I'll tell them I'm up for it.' Lee passed him his coat. In the hood, his face looked smaller and less confident. Lee kissed his cheek.

When he forced the front door open, the car was waiting in the same place. The roadway was papered with snow.

White flakes were drifting out of the night. He closed the door with his shoulder and returned to the sofa and the whisky bottle.

The next day, Lee phoned the agency and fixed up the date. Then he e-mailed Ben: *Weird card you sent. The sun setting behind a forest in winter. Where did you find it?* The rest of the day was spent buying a few gifts for his sister and their children; he was seeing them for lunch on Boxing Day. The day after, he was visiting Jason. On Christmas Day, apart from a lunchtime drink with some friends, he'd be at home. He selected a bottle of Laphroaig for then.

It was already dark when he got home, and a near-freezing rain had washed away the traces of snow. Once again, the front door resisted him. He didn't feel at home here. It was time to move on. After pouring himself a glass of Black Bush, Lee switched on his computer. There was a reply from Ben: *Sorry, I don't remember that card. Are you sure it was from me? I thought I'd sent you one with meercats wearing Santa hats.*

Suddenly feeling very tired, Lee put his glass down and checked through the text messages on his phone. They would all need acting on tomorrow. Work accumulated, you could never put it aside for long.

Snow had turned the landscape into a dream. Lee drove up through the city centre to the Hockley Flyover and on past futuristic superstores and derelict factories. Only the faces of buildings stood out from the featureless white, like images adrift on a screen of static. Even in the car, he could feel the chill of frozen ground. The satnav was unable to identify his destination; it kept telling him to go back to the city centre. He had to rely on the local map, and even that seemed to be out of date. Where there should be narrow streets, there were only tower blocks and car parks. Most of the traffic was lorries passing through, driving slowly to avoid skidding. He was in danger of being late: the agency had told him four o'clock, and it was ten to. The light was thinning, but the streetlamps hadn't come on yet.

At last he saw the name of the road he needed to follow into the estate where Jason lived. It led between huge unlit buildings and over a frozen canal. He needed the third side-road on the left. As he turned, the roadway dipped and he cut deep into a bank of snow. There was no way forward, and the wheels slipped when he tried to reverse. Lee gave up and killed the engine, then got out, clutching a net-wrapped bottle of Cabernet Sauvignon. He walked cautiously, afraid of falling in his best jeans and brown leather jacket. This was a thrill he rarely allowed himself: to visit a rent boy on his home ground, to share his living space, see his wall posters, lie on his single bed.

No car had driven along this road since the snowfall, and the footing was treacherous. Lee shivered. The houses were narrow three-storey terraces of the kind that had mostly been demolished around here. Some of the doorways were bricked up or boarded over. The road curved, and the shadows deepened. At last he got to the right house and rang the bell for Flat 3. The door was painted a dark blue. There was no sound from inside. He waited, then rang again. The door swung right open, and two men came out with a third following. None of them was Jason. Lee was backing off but the snow on the path impeded him. He dropped the bottle. It didn't break, which gave him the sense of being in a dream. The nearest man whipped something from his pocket that glittered in the fading light. Lee turned and tried to run. The three men came after him, blocking the way back to his car. They were silent. He staggered further up the narrow road with the men in pursuit.

Nobody else was about, no traffic, no lights on in the tall houses. Maybe if he could get further ahead, he could hide somewhere and they wouldn't see him. But it was hard to keep moving when the snow numbed his feet. He didn't know who they were – somebody's brothers or friends, it didn't matter. He wasn't going to join their Facebook group. Lee was breathing hard now, sweating despite the chill. His legs ached. The sameness of inert houses and cars surrounding him, the snow everywhere tinged with dirt, made him feel there was nowhere to go. He couldn't escape the feeling that he'd known this would happen. It had been a statement that it would, not a question of whether it might.

At last the road came to an end. There was a factory with dull blue light in its windows, but the gate was locked. A dog barked as he struggled onward, his movement reduced to a cartoon slowness by the snow. Then a railway bridge with a light beyond it – maybe a station, or a courtyard with a brazier, or a hostel. Dream on. He ran under the bridge and tripped on something under the snow, almost fell. They caught him there. A foot kicked him low in the stomach, and he screamed but heard no sound. A hand unzipped his jacket, a surprisingly gentle act. He saw the knife coming down and twisted aside. It punched under his ribs, then slid out. The blood was comfortably warm. It stained the snow like tar. The three men were still now, watching him. Lee rose to his feet. His own breath was freezing on his lips. It was only a flesh wound, but they didn't know that. Pressing a hand to the tender heat in his side, he walked on.

There were no buildings, only trees with the light beyond them. This must be a park. He could see thin figures like meercats drifting between the trees. Lee recognised their faces, but they didn't notice him, or they ignored him. The shadows under the trees were blue. As he stumbled onward, a branch lashed out and cut his hand. He passed another tree and felt it slash his cheek. All the trees had razors, he realised. How many more did he have to get past? He suspected he wouldn't reach the light. But there was only one way to find out.

A FARAWAY CITY

It wasn't just a bad dream. Kathy was used to those. They had their own shut-in logic of failure and humiliation. Getting arrested while on holiday with Steve, for a long-past crime that she'd forgotten. Being trapped in the office lift all night long and found by her colleagues in the morning. Needing to pee on a Tube train that was stuck in a tunnel. Cooking a whole salmon for a dinner party and finding its interior was swollen with black fungus. Those were bad dreams. This was something different. Something that woke her up three times, sweating, her eyelids sticky with tears. The third time, she had to run to the bathroom and vomit.

Steve was deep in the cocoon of his own profound sleep, a low-key snore distorting his breath. She badly needed some normality, but she didn't wake him up. Sounds and images played over and over in her head. *A fist smashing into her eye. A man's face, twisted with rage. A black van full of silent women.*

Blood in a toilet pan. A gaunt, unpainted tower block. Pockmarked walls. A hand slapping her mouth, loosening some teeth. Three naked men waiting for her to suck them. And the words, hissed or shouted in her ear, she didn't know the language, but she understood what they were telling her. *You're a whore. You've got it coming, bitch. You're dead. Shut the fuck up. Die.*

It wasn't just a bad dream. It was *someone else's* bad dream. This wasn't her life given a degrading twist. It was someone else trapped in a place where the worst kind of degradation was normal. There was no waking up. But she was awake – at least, she hoped she was. The alarm clock said it was ten minutes to six. Kathy had a three-hour meeting today to plan the new marketing campaign. Lack of sleep was not appropriate. But she lay awake, trembling, until the alarm went off.

———————

Steve wasn't his real name. He'd told her before they were married. 'I need a modern name. A smooth name, with no crap hanging off it. Gerard Temple isn't me. Took me thirty years to realise, but I'm not that. I can tell you what Steve Temple is doing, where he's going, what he brings in. It's the name of a player.'

They'd been together for six years. Neither of them was keen to have children. They'd both worked their way up in the soft furnishings industry, late career developers, just starting to make it at the time when the former bright young things were looking to factor in babies and work-life balance. Their elegant Chelsea home required them both to be not just earning, but winning.

Not wanting to start a family didn't mean they weren't passionate. One of Kathy's worries, after eight or nine of the alien nightmares, was that the abuse she was dreaming would somehow make her damaged goods. There was desire in her normal dreams, but it wasn't consummated. Would Steve know she'd been raped in her recent dreams? If so, was it her fault? That wasn't a simple question. It wasn't like she'd been raped in real life. Even though, night after night, she was running to the bathroom to vomit. Feeling the after-effects of an unreal violation.

The nightmares came every week. Usually after Steve had been away on a sales trip. Oddly, Kathy didn't dream in his absence. As soon as he was curled up beside her, snoring gently, his sperm delivered between her thighs, the terror came. The battered, cheaply made blocks. The vans and lorries that took frightened women through cities choked with traffic. The dark-haired men who used her viciously, or at best while locked into a bad dream of their own. Was this Eastern Europe? It wasn't anywhere she knew. And the language of what the men said to her peeled away from its meaning like a used condom.

The nightmares were a feathered cry from some part of herself she didn't recognise, now or in the past. Kathy was still wondering how to tell Steve about them when she found his notebook.

They'd been to visit friends, the night before, and Steve had drunk a little more wine than was good for him. First the clumsy innuendoes and the rants against 'health and safety fascists', then the flushed face and the dry-heaving in the street. Kathy had helped him undress, though she'd drawn the line at his drowsy attempt to make love. 'The drink talking is bad enough,' she'd told him. To make it worse, she'd been quite in the mood – but not for his boozy groping and slobbering.

In the morning, he'd left early to get to a meeting in Richmond. Hung over more by lack of sleep than by alcohol, Kathy had chosen to work from home. And just as she couldn't start work in the morning without tidying her desk, she couldn't switch on her laptop until the house was in some kind of order. On the bedroom floor, she'd noticed a tiny key that Steve must have dropped when changing his trousers. The key to his laptop? If so, he'd surely come back. She took the key into Steve's cluttered study. Then she saw the tiny locked drawer on the right-hand side of the desk.

The notebook was slim, bound in calf leather, with white unruled pages. It was three-quarters full of notes in Steve's tiny print. His pen had scored deep into the paper. Each page was headlined with a name. *Emma, Tina, Sarah, Linda.* The most English of names, bland as afternoon tea. Under each name was a detailed account of how he had visited each woman, given her money and had sex with her. More often than not, extra services had been required. Every time, he'd noted the girl's ethnic background: *Russian, Czech, Romanian, Polish.* Their names weren't real any more than his name was. Any more than his marriage was.

The descriptions stuck in her mind: a mixture of boyish excitement and cool, businesslike acronyms. 'VFM' was familiar from the office, of course; but if 'CIM' didn't mean the Chartered Institute of Marketing (and it probably didn't), what did it mean? When she realised, she had to drop the book and run once more to the bathroom to be sick. When she came back, she went on reading. The firm spikes and curves of his writing took on a sexual meaning to her. All of it hard and intense, none of it joined up.

There was a date at the end of each narrative – the last nine were this year. And it was only March. Some of the dates coincided with Steve's business trips, but some were just normal working days. Ones when he'd stayed late or driven out to a meeting. After each date was an initial or pair of initials: *MM, K, RX*. The names of brothels? There were no details of locations. The encounters could have happened in office cubicles.

Kathy locked the desk drawer, but kept the notebook. She poured herself a glass of brandy and drank it in two gulps. Switched on her laptop, but couldn't focus on the screen. Washed her glass in the sink, accidentally broke it against the tap, cut the tip of her finger, held it under cold water until her hand was white. Began to scream, but stopped when she heard herself. Sat down and cried, then stopped crying. Waited. Afraid to go to sleep in case another dream broke in.

Steve came back late, in a foul mood. He slammed the door and announced to Kathy: 'You wouldn't believe what happened this afternoon. Three hours pissed up the wall because some interfering government inspector decided to waste our time. If I run into him on a dark night, he'd better watch his own fucking health and safety, that's all.' He took off his jacket, gave Kathy a swift kiss and shot her one of his practised I-feel-your-pain looks. 'How was your day, love?'

Kathy handed him the notebook. 'You'd better take this. Record your after-work adventures before you forget the details.'

'Where did you get this?' Steve rubbed the leather binding with his fingertips as if he'd never touched it before.

'You dropped the key.'

Steve looked up, dismay written across his broad face. 'I thought we both believed in personal privacy. Now you raid my desk like some official from the local council, or some child who can't keep her hand out of other people's—'

'It's where you've put *your* hand that bothers me,' Kathy shouted. 'And where you've put something else. It's all there. You *bastard*.' Her voice broke. She turned away, putting a hand to her mouth. The light in the room seemed to waver; darkness pressed in from outside, flooding the house.

Steve moved behind her and gripped her arms, very gently, like the brother she'd lost in her teens. 'Darling, I never did any of those things. I've been writing porn for a webzine. It's a shameful hobby, and I didn't have the courage to tell you, but that's all it is. Just a part of my imagination that's still sixteen. I've never paid for sex. Why should I have to?' He kissed her cheek. 'Can you forgive me?'

'Why are you obsessed with Eastern European girls?' she asked, still looking away from him. Her own voice sounded to her like a ghost.

'The man in the stories is a character, not me. He's a wanderer. I'm not. I know where I belong. And besides, you know how I feel about immigrants. Do you really think I'm capable of that?'

Kathy didn't answer, and he seemed to take that as a sign of acceptance. He poured them both a glass of wine, and they had a fairly normal evening. The darkness stayed outside the walls. She caught up with some of the work she'd left undone in the day, and he finished the wine while watching a DVD. They went to bed a little earlier than usual, and Steve was unusually tender with her. Kathy wondered if he was thinking about his English-named girls, real or imagined. She tried not to think about them, but the dreams were harder to forget than the notebook. At the climax of her latest dream, her voice was shadowed by a hidden cry of fear.

The unreality was growing. Shopping for lunch at Waitrose, Kathy felt trapped in a model village: organic vegetables and raw seafood declaring a rural identity the shoppers would never touch. For a while she had no idea how to get out: the roads all ended in walls. Drinking with a few colleagues in a bar on the Embankment after work, she experienced a partial loss of sight. Her glass, the optics and the windows were filled with unreflecting darkness. She got her assistant to drive her home.

That night, the worst dream yet. She woke drenched with sweat, feeling a sick headache start even as the pain of the raw dream-injuries faded. A dull ache in the pit of her stomach told her she'd come on a few days early. Chaotic images pressed behind her eyes: a private party where she was viciously beaten by three other girls, one of them using a broken bottle to draw the letter S on her back. A dozen or so men in business suits, watching.

And then she was in a clinic, giving birth to the child of a nameless man. Passing out from loss of blood, coming round to find the baby had been taken away. They'd only let her have the child because of the money she could bring in when pregnant. Holding onto the grief, because at least that, if nothing else in the dream, was human.

Steve was fast asleep. It was an hour before dawn. Kathy slipped out of the bed and walked unsteadily to the bathroom, where she pulled off her sweat-soaked nightdress and washed herself until she recognised her own body. She felt weak, drained of hope and purpose. Was that how it felt when your dreams were replaced with someone else's memories? The prospect of a day at work, or even at home, seemed unreal to her.

She couldn't face either dressing or getting back into bed. Instead, she slipped into the fluffy white dressing-gown she'd bought herself years ago, and went through to her own cubicle-sized study. If she could find Steve's online erotic fantasies, that would help put her mind at rest. Maybe it would all be resolved by the time he woke up. Google searches for *Eastern European girls* and a few other strategic keywords revealed no pornographic writings, though it did bring up a few London massage parlours. That made her stop and think, her back aching from the hard chair, before refocusing her search.

On a website dedicated to customer reviews of prostitutes, she found a database whose subject fields included 'name of girl', 'location' and 'reviewer'. Kathy was impressed by the site's IT infrastructure, but that wasn't foremost in her mind. It took her less than ten minutes to find a chain of reviews, by someone called 'the wanderer', of encounters with Russian, Czech, Polish and Romanian girls who had names like Jane, Kate and Lucy – scattered over the UK, but mostly in South London. She read nine of them. They were already familiar to her.

By the time Steve woke up, Kathy was already dressed and getting ready for work. She kissed him, put a mug of coffee on the sideboard for him, said nothing about the website. It had only confirmed what she'd known since finding his notebook. He wasn't real any more. What was, she still had to find out.

———————

The parlour was in Croydon. When Kathy had phoned, the receptionist – a young woman with a marked, possibly deliberate South London accent – had said, 'It'll cost extra.' She'd asked for Susan. That was the last of the wanderer's reviews. The last entry in the notebook.

'That'll be fine,' the voice had said, then paused. 'Tell you what, darling. You don't want to come here. There's a hotel up the road, we can book a room for you. Just go in half an hour before your appointment time, pay for the room, go up there and call us. We'll sort out the rest.'

It was a Friday afternoon. For all Steve knew, she was at work. The hotel, not surprisingly, was a fleapit that probably made most of its cash from hourly bookings. She checked in under her maiden name. The room, on the third floor, had grey flocked wallpaper and a brass dado rail that ended at the black-painted partition wall. At least the single bed had a fresh duvet cover.

Kathy had read in a newspaper that three-quarters of

prostitutes in the UK had been trafficked. Many of the rest had come from overseas of their own accord. What were they running from? Not communism, not any more. She recalled one of Steve's wine-fuelled monologues over the table: 'The laws of the economy can't be changed. What we have to do is guarantee individual freedom.' But he didn't want them coming here. Or did he? Kathy stared out of the window at the broken skyline. Trying to abort the images that flooded behind her eyes. Nothing felt real. The girl she was waiting for would take her back into an unknown city. She was caught between worlds.

There was a quiet knock at the door. Kathy let in a short, dark-haired girl in a long fabric coat. 'Hello, I'm Susan.' Under the make-up, her face was as blank as an Expressionist sketch: a ghost of the living. She unbuttoned the coat to reveal a black slip and miniskirt, then asked for the money. Kathy paid her. 'What do you want?' the girl asked.

'Sit here and I'll tell you.' She pointed to the bed. With the self-possession of a wounded cat, the girl perched on the blue duvet and waited. Kathy sat beside her and pressed a hand to her back, just above the shoulder. The scar was there, as she'd known it would be. She remembered the words in Steve's notebook: *Central European, from one of those old countries that surfaced after liberation.*

Kathy's fingers brushed the girl's cheek. Felt her sudden tension. 'I want you to give me my dreams back,' she said.

Susan looked at her with eyes that were broken windows. 'Do dreams belong to anyone?'

'They do. And so do memories.'

'I can't help you.' The girl drew away from Kathy's embrace. 'Don't know anything. There's not just you. Not just me. Everything…' She was crying. 'Fuck this. Fuck. Fuck.' Her thin hands gripped her face.

Kathy turned, feeling as if a breeze might tear the fragile girl in half, and hugged her awkwardly. Susan muttered, 'Do what you want.'

'Tell me something,' Kathy said. 'What's your real name?'

There was maybe a minute's silence before the girl wiped her eyes and said: 'I don't know. Maybe I never had one.'

The airport was a model city with its own shops and bars and cafes, its own buses carrying people from one crowded place to another. Except that no one lived here. The traveller waiting to check in glanced at her passport, as if trying to memorise her own name. The photograph didn't look much like her. She'd packed overnight, while Steve was away on a business trip, taking only her everyday clothes and a few necessities. How long would it take him to realise she wasn't coming back?

It was nearly four a.m. The airport windows were painted with darkness. The people around her had the window-dummy faces of the unslept. She didn't want to sleep again, though obviously she'd have to. The queue brought her to the check-in point and she handed over her suitcases. They felt as light as her passport.

On the way to customs, she saw a group of young men and women with narrow faces and dark eyes, tired but restless, heading for the exit. They were huddled together, but not speaking or looking at each other. None of them was holding a cigarette, but a whitish mist was drifting from their mouths and nostrils.

She walked on to the restless queue at the checkpoint. Businessmen heading for conferences. Wealthy couples going on holiday. The man in front of her was sharing his impatience with a flattened phone. 'Airports are a living hell,' he said. She laughed. Had these people ever been her kind?

Soon the narrow plane was drifting in a pure white city of clouds. Was it only the view that made her feel so cold? She wondered briefly how Steve was taking advantage of his trip, whether he was visiting someone from the city she was flying to. But he didn't seem real to her now. It wasn't what he'd done that had made her take this flight. It was the girls with their English names, their violent dreams, the ruined but populated city they had flown out of.

Eventually, she slept. And woke sweating, confused and sick, not knowing what she'd dreamed. A man with stubble on his narrow face. A black powder burning on crumpled foil, its cold smoke bringing her into a place of stillness, a sleep within sleep, a place where nothing could hurt her. Not even the bleeding she could feel inside. Her eyes opened and she saw the interior of the plane, but now it seemed ancient and frozen like an underground cave.

He was waiting at the airport, on his own. They sat in the bar and drank black coffee. The need was hollowing out her bones. Her face was a mask of sweat. The coffee burned her mouth, but she hardly felt it. 'I'll call you Katrina,' he said. 'Because you'll make a flood.' She nodded, barely listening. *How long?*

'You're older than most of the girls,' he was saying. 'That means you have to do something none of them will do. It's very easy. I'll provide the men. All you have to do is be dead for them.' He looked at her in the way someone had a lifetime ago when he'd wanted her to know he was sincere. She smiled.

'I'll give you something to knock you out. You won't feel a thing. You'll be away in dreamland. Wake up a bit torn, but what's new?'

'Can I have some now?' she asked.

His face hardened. 'Not here, it's too obvious. Soon. My flat's only a few miles away. Maybe we can have a rehearsal. I could do with some relaxation, Katrina. It's been a long day.'

He took her arm and guided her calmly, almost tenderly, towards the concrete tunnel where the taxis waited. As she perched on the hard seat and the cab jerked forward into streets that looked unfinished in the frail sodium light, a nest of concrete fragments on a mountainside in a permanent night, she had the momentary sensation of another life slipping beyond her reach. A life that she'd missed. But anyone would feel the same. And it meant nothing: she couldn't break free.

Not on her own.

THE WILLOW PATTERN

A few days into the new year, Richard's father phoned me. We'd only met once, five years before, so I knew it wasn't a social call. He told me Richard was dead. 'He had an accident while suffering from depression.' I asked what had happened. 'He took too many sleeping pills. He was drunk. No letter or anything.' I said I was sorry. 'I know you and he split up. But your name was still in his address book. I wondered if you'd like to come to the funeral.' I said yes, and thanked him for getting in touch. When I put the phone down, the flat seemed colder than before. Light was shifting in the sky, as if on the surface of water. I went to find Carl. He was in the kitchen, cooking. I told him what had happened. He embraced me without saying anything.

The funeral was in Macclesfield, where Richard's parents lived now. A metallic, functional town. I sat uneasily through a service Richard would have detested, in a grey church where light sifted the dust high overhead. Lack of sleep made my own grief feel heavy and impersonal, like a cold. I felt that I'd already mourned his loss, years before. His death made me feel hopeless, not bereaved. At the graveside, there seemed to be a disproportionate number of male relatives – possibly cousins – who looked like younger versions of Richard. The sky was overcast and brittle. The empty grave made me think of a cavity in a row of teeth. I didn't stay long at the reception. Being Richard's ex-lover would have been awkward at the best of times. I shook his father's hand; his mother kissed me on the cheek.

Afterwards, I wondered why none of our mutual friends from the old days had been at the funeral. Maybe Richard had lost touch with them. But hadn't he lost touch with me? The next couple of weeks were pretty hectic at work, which stopped me brooding over it. The company had committed itself to a huge range of new products, and I had to design all the catalogue pages and leaflets. I was working into the evenings, sometimes coming home to find Carl had already gone out. I hadn't told him much about Richard. In my experience, it's better not to lay chapter and verse regarding your exes on a new lover. Even one who's moved in with you.

What happened then was partly due to work pressure. I'd been drinking late, vodka, to help me get to sleep. One Friday morning, I heard the alarm nagging through a haze of deferred stillness. Despite the cold, I was sweating. Taking care not to wake Carl, who didn't need to get up for a while, I slipped out of bed and put on my dressing-gown. Then I went into the kitchen, put the kettle on and made some breakfast. I was drinking coffee and wondering whether the post had come when I glanced at the timer on the video. It was seven minutes past four. I was almost three hours ahead of myself. For the first time I registered that it was that much darker, that much colder, than even a typical January morning. Perhaps the video was wrong. I crept back into the bedroom and checked the alarm clock. It showed ten past four, and was set to go off at seven. I hadn't switched it off.

Carl and I didn't get out much. Living and sleeping together was as much of each other's company as we needed. He was a quiet lad, with close-cropped hair and eyes that seemed to reach back into the night. There was something inarticulate and physical about him that coloured our relationship. I remember the first time we went to bed: how he curled up under me, pulling his knees up to his chest, and drew me into him until we formed the two halves of a closed shell; how he gripped my hand and moved it from place to place on his body; how his dead eyes opened and stared through me as we shuddered together. Soon after that, we both had blood tests and, on getting a negative result, started having unprotected sex. I'd never done that with Richard, because he'd never been faithful to me for long enough.

The sleepwalking incidents got worse. Nearly every night I woke up out of bed – curled up on the floor in the freezing bathroom, on the sofa in front of a blank TV screen, standing at the front door trying to find the keys in my pyjamas. I'd always double-locked that door for safety; now it had the added purpose of keeping me in. There was nothing very strange about my dreams. I was always just going about my life, getting up, preparing to go out. I was expecting to see someone. When I woke up, it was like falling out of normality into a damaged world. The pattern breaking up. Maybe I was getting out of bed so I could wake up alone and cold. Once or twice, I felt a pressure in the air, a stillness, and wondered if God was about to speak to me. I don't believe in God, but that was how it felt. The intake of breath before the words came.

One Sunday afternoon in late January, I decided to walk into town along the canalside. Carl was away visiting his sister. He didn't like walks anyway. It had been a freezing night, mist stuck hard to the windows; but today the sun was shining through a glassy layer of sky. The canal walkway began in Yardley, opposite a Victorian cemetery full of milky-white angels. The water surface was frozen over, a faint pattern of ridges turning the ice into a pavement. On the far side of the canal, the backs of derelict factories had been sprayed with Technicolor graffiti designs: soft letters, clouds, lightning bolts. The glass in the high windows was broken, revealing darkness. On the path side, leafless trees were etched against a blank sky. I had a chill from the night, a nasty cold coming on. But I kept walking.

Why had Richard died? It didn't sound like an accident. But I couldn't believe he'd gone out hating life or himself. He wasn't like that. He enjoyed his own pain too much. It had to be something unbearable, something in particular. Like AIDS or cancer. But if his family had known anything, they hadn't told me. It wasn't like I had a right to know. I was only his ex. We'd hardly spoken in three years. My strongest images of him were from the early days, back in college. And the nights. Walking up the long, straight Manchester streets, across the parks, litter poltergeisting around us. The subways, the canals. Kissing against a wall in the golden streetlight. Richard's mouth open, his long hair breaking up around his face.

Further along the canal, a ruined doorway in the brickwork led through into a disused factory yard. Several rotten doors lay face down on the frozen mud, grass stretched across their glass like wire. Scraps of wallpaper and torn-off paint were grafted onto the uneven dirt. As if someone had dreamed a house and let it decay as only dreams can. I took a few cautious steps beyond the doorway, then crouched and blinked at the eroded concrete walls. Suddenly my eyes were flooding and I couldn't move.

Richard was one of the first friends I made at university. We used to meet up between lectures, go to the bookshop or the record shop together. On his own he'd always wear a concealed Walkman. The Doors, the Velvet Underground, the Bunnymen. He usually wore a black denim jacket which matched his hair. Early on, we kept running into each other at the same societies or events: concerts, films, a Poll Tax demo, a lecture on telepathy, a performance of Pinter's *Betrayal*. One evening I cooked dinner for him. We shared two bottles of red wine. It got too late for him to leave, since his lodgings were a bus ride away. No confessions or seductions were needed: we made love. I wasn't his first partner, but I was the first boy to fuck him. That happened a few weeks later, on his red duvet in sunlight. He gave it to me too. Strange how these things can give a framework to your life. I didn't just need any more. I belonged.

It was too early, of course. In more ways than one. As we grew up, we broke the chrysalis of our imagined twinship. But it lasted four years, on and off, well into the first year of real life. We even lived together for a while, and spent a week camping in the hills of North Wales. Those platform shoes were a disaster on muddy ground. We shared music, politics, a love of bass notes and darkened rooms and plain chocolate. We walked home along busy streets in the early hours of the morning, holding hands. We were so close that sex between us felt like masturbation, like incest. Richard used to say that we belonged together without needing to behave like a couple. He was right. That was the problem.

Maybe what he wanted with me was more than love. He was heavily into astrology and fringe religion at that time. We both joined a parapsychology group and spent many pointless evenings sitting round ouija boards or trying to project images under Ganzfeld conditions. None of it ever worked. But he used to talk about sharing dreams, touching the astral body with the fingers of the mind. We never did meet in a dream, not really. Once I dreamt I was following him through a wood. I could see his naked back and arse moving in front of me, but when I reached out all I could feel was wet bark. The sound of rain blurred my voice, like static on a radio, and he didn't hear me. Richard's dreams often had to do with canals. Him trying to dredge furniture from the mud under yards of still water. Old chairs, beds, sofas. He'd get stuck trying to pull something free of the weeds, start drowning and wake up in a cold sweat. He wanted me to help him release the memories. I understand that now.

He was always in search of new experiences, whether physical or mental. Sometimes he'd go into the city alone and just explore – maybe spend the night at a rave, which was quite a new thing then, high on speed or E. Maybe get sucked off in a park or an alley in the dead hours between clubtime and dawn. He told me things a few times, but I made him stop. Sometimes there were marks, bruises or bites. In retaliation I went out with other blokes, usually students. But we always came back to each other. One night I walked him along ten miles of canal walkway between Manchester and Stockport. He'd been smoking heroin and was in danger of passing out. It was a June night, but Richard was shivering. 'Are you cold?' I kept asking him. He said, 'I'm cold inside.' When we finally got home, I undressed him and let him fall through my arms into his static, waterlogged dreams. Richard wasn't into drugs. They made him panicky and ill, and he never got addicted. Except to alcohol, of course. That was something we had in common. Neither of us could get along with people who didn't drink.

Richard eventually left me for a woman. Or rather, his affair with her made me leave *him*. I'd never seen him in love with someone else before. It made me wonder if he'd ever loved me. They were only together a few months, but by then I'd moved to Birmingham and decided I didn't want him back. We stayed in touch, by phone mostly. Over the next couple of years he made several attempts at going steady with men or women, but it never lasted. He was too intense in some ways, too careless in others. From a friend in Manchester I heard about him sometimes turning up drunk in Rocky's nightclub and trying to pick up the drag queens, a quick shot of quasi-hetero sex. Even his ambiguity he wanted given to him on a plate.

As I stood there in the derelict yard, sunlight wriggling in a net of cloud overhead, one particular story came back to me. It was something he'd told me from his childhood. I went back onto the canal towpath and walked on towards Small Heath, thinking about it. The light traced patterns of flaws and ridges on the ice surface; they seemed regular and abstract, like the image of a perfect world. Then I came to a bridge that had been designed to contain a fan of granite supports, with the bricks worked in above them. The granite pieces were too long; the builder had cut the ends off some of them, and made the bricks fit using odd pieces of brick and lots of mortar. It was a hideously botched job, despite the elegance of the design. I smiled, and felt Richard laugh quietly inside me. The sky was clearing.

He couldn't have been older than nine. It was a bank holiday, probably Easter; the morning had been bright and cold. Richard's father had gone out to visit a friend for a game of chess. After lunch, his mother put on her make-up and jacket. 'Come on, Richard. Let's go out for a walk before your father gets back.' They took the bus out of town, to an area Richard hadn't seen before. Streets of terraced houses broke up around factories and tower blocks. When they got off the bus, his mother held Richard's hand tightly. She was wearing thin leather gloves. Her face was set hard, even paler than usual. A patch of wasteground by the side of the road was heaped with refuse, mostly food cartons and bottles. All the flats behind it were derelict, their windows either boarded up or smashed in; except for two flats which had curtains and washing lines, and flowers in their window-boxes. 'Poor sods,' his mother said. 'Why do they hang on? They're as crazy as the vandals.'

The sun came out, breaking the pale sky into silver-edged pieces. A high brick wall surrounded the local reservoir; the gates at the near end were open. They walked across a bridge where, obviously, there had been a fight and it hadn't rained since. Dried blood was spattered across the tarmac surface and hand-smeared on the wooden rail facing the water. Down on the footpath, weeds and rushes were mixed with normal grass and shrubbery. You could still see the grey factory chimneys smoking above the trees. Richard's mother stared at the water surface. Her eyes were wide, as if trying to collect every scrap of light. When Richard looked at the water, he imagined the sky was down there and felt momentarily dizzy.

At the far end of the reservoir, the bank was a flat marsh streaked with red clay; the water was black. Richard's mother let go of his hand and stood looking at something close by. There were tears on her face. Her arms, crossed over, were shaking. Richard tried to see what she was looking at. He couldn't see anything there except a willow tree, its lowest twigs reaching the ground. It trembled slightly, like its own reflection in the still water. Eventually, his mother walked on, and Richard followed until she turned and took his hand again. There was another gate at this end, leading back onto the main road.

When they got back to the house, Richard's father greeted them with a frozen stare. 'Where the fuck have you been? I've telephoned the police and all the hospitals.'

She stared back at him, then laughed quietly. 'No, you haven't. Don't be childish. You're trying to make him afraid of me, aren't you?'

'Don't laugh at me, you bitch.' A few seconds of stillness; then his mother walked upstairs to the bedroom and slammed the door. It was a typically blank, impenetrable ending to the trip.

In that year there'd been a number of fights. They often tried to ignore each other, but that was impossible at night. Sometimes they'd sleep in separate rooms and end up going back and forth to shout at each other. Once he tried to drag her downstairs from the bathroom; at the top of the stairs, she scratched his face, and he staggered all the way down backwards, wiping the blood from his cheek onto the handrail.

Another time, years earlier, Richard's mother threw a set of ornamental plates at the living room wall – one by one, lifting *them slowly back. For weeks, pieces of the willow pattern etched into the plates kept turning up in corners and behind the furniture. There was one plate left, standing in the cabinet, undamaged.*

Stories within stories. Dreams within dreams. The cold caught up with me after that walk. I tried to fight it off with paracetamol, but it sank from my head down into my chest and hung there. Pressure of schedules kept me at work, coughing in feverish spasms that made the words dance on the little computer screen. By the end of the week, my lungs felt like wads of tissue paper. I was sleeping so badly that Carl, on my insistence, relocated to the futon in the living room.

One of those nights, I dreamt I was a canal. Locked in by stone, unable to move, I felt something move inside me. It shifted around, freeing itself, then slowly came to the surface. I saw a hand without fingers, a tongueless open mouth. As it crawled across the bed and the towpath, I saw it was a sleeping child. Then I woke up and the room was dark. Something moved off the edge of the bed and fell clumsily. It was more than an hour before I could find the courage to switch on the bedside lamp. The child was slumped in the corner, watching me with eyes of mud. He was three or four years old, naked, his skin a pale shade of grey. I couldn't hear him breathing. After a while I fell asleep with the lamp still on.

The child didn't go away, but he moved about. Sometimes he was in the bathroom, hugging the radiator with his large flat hands. Sometimes he was in the hall, as if waiting to be let out; when I opened the front door, he didn't move. Usually he was in the bedroom, somewhere just at the edge of my view. By daylight or full electric light he was translucent, the way a baby's ear or finger-webs can be. You could see the light through him, but nothing else. He reminded me of photographs of myself as an infant, walking along low walls in Leicester. Carl didn't seem to notice him. I tried not to.

That weekend, Carl and I got drunk on red wine and lay together in the living room, half on the futon and half on the floor. Apart from the gas fire, the only light was the red signal on the stereo. The long drum rolls of Gallon Drunk's 'In the Long Still Night' shuddered around us, the slow piano chords giving an undertone of fragile tenderness. We undressed each other and floated in a haze of fatigue and desire, exploring patiently with our hands and mouths. He asked me to fuck him. I spread his body out beneath me, my face beside his, and felt him press up as I entered him from behind. My hand stroked his lower belly, then gripped his cock. A dark heat spread from my chest into my face, and I tasted blood on my upper lip. I couldn't stop; it was like being a passenger in myself. As I reached the climax, blood poured from my nose onto Carl's shoulders. I hoped he'd forgive me. The combined effect of sex, fever and loss of blood made me come like never before. For a few seconds I couldn't move. Blood trickled into my mouth and I nearly choked. Then I lifted myself, pulled away from Carl and took a deep painful breath.

Carl didn't move. 'Are you okay?' I said. No answer. I stood up and reached for a box of tissues, to clean the blood from his neck and shoulders. Cold pressed in around the gas fire's nest of warmth. Something crept from behind the futon into the shadows. I bunched a mass of white tissues in my hand and knelt beside Carl. The blood had eaten through to the shoulder blades, exposing the pale

47

knobs of his spine. Where I'd coughed over his ear, only a ragged fin was left. I dropped the tissues against the back of his ribcage. Already he was losing shape, blurring into the dark fabric of the futon. When there was nothing left but a charcoal sketch in the air, a folded shadow, I turned the gas fire off and went to bed.

I lay there in the dark, redrafting my memory. It was like waking from a dream and not knowing quite how things stand. Had this been going on for weeks? Or had it begun and ended now, and all memories of going out with Carl and living with him were false? But not even mortal terror can keep a man awake after sex. I fell asleep and didn't wake up until early dawn, when something else was trying to pull away from me. He was nearly my own height, a teenager, a thin double. I heard him sleepwalking around the flat, blundering softly into things.

The next night, it was a newborn baby. I could just feel his soft breath on my fingertips. Since he couldn't move around by himself, I picked him up and put him in the empty cat basket. I was between cats. His eyes didn't open, but I could see the eyeballs moving under the whitish lids. On Monday morning I woke up with all three of them around me. The baby at the foot of the bed, the child perched on the windowsill, the adolescent sitting at the bookshelf and leafing through a book without seeing it. Being unable to wake up was not enough to keep them still.

Then I thought of Richard's funeral, and the penny finally dropped. Again I felt that stillness in the air, like the pause before someone begins to speak. It was such a waste. A terrible, miraculous waste. He'd broken through after all. But somehow we'd not been in touch, and it was too late. A few words from either of us – a phone call, a visit – might have made all the difference.

I keep a baseball bat near the bed in case of a break-in. That morning, I destroyed the sleepwalkers with it. The teenager first, then the infant, then the baby. They had no bones or flesh, only form, and their bodies quickly dried out once broken. I gathered the brittle husks in a bin liner and kicked it until it was nearly flat. Then I carried it out to the row of dustbins at the side of the building. The way they had cracked apart made me feel awful. But memories have a lifespan, like anything else. Sometimes you have to help them die.

Outside in the street, people were on their way to work. I could see their paths intersecting, weaving around each other, making patterns. Was any pattern real or just something imposed by human need? All the patterns of Richard, the contradictions, the duality, came down to one final paradox. Richard's absence was all I had of him. Once I stopped missing him, he'd be gone.

ECHOLAND

Moth had fans now, a chosen few. At least half a dozen in the audience, probably all students, wearing the silver on black T-shirt they'd been selling at the last gig. Just before the band started, Diane went out for a breath of fresh air. The Victorian church at the centre of St Peter's Square was closed up and unlit; she stood in its doorway, sheltering from the invisible rain. Up towards the city centre, streetlights glimmered like faint candles. Behind her, the locked door smelt of damp. She loved doorways, but they never let her through. Lighting a cigarette, she sucked deep and breathed a grey veil over her face, then dropped the tiny flame and ground it out with her left boot.

Matt had a bottle of Corona ready for her on stage. Diane suspected the singer had a slight crush on her. Was that why Tara, who was currently stamping tiny red moths on people's hands, wouldn't give her the time of day? Not that Diane cried herself to sleep over it. Matt's bass was already blending with Ian's drums as she strapped on her guitar and gulped a sharp mouthful of beer. The audience were swaying gently in the twilight, only their faces visible.

She cut her finger on the first chord, played on regardless, the jagged melody giving Matt's harsh voice something to work against. His lyrics were a blend of New Age mysticism and second-hand depression, but if you couldn't hear the words it all made sense. The song built up into a pulsing storm of riffs and beats, then faded to a single repeated chord. Diane licked the blood from her finger and drowned the taste with beer. Matt introduced the next song: 'This is for Tara.' A morbidly romantic piece that gave Diane less to do. Resisting the impulse to mime being sick, she looked out over the blurred faces of the audience. Faint red lights trembled in the distance.

As the applause faded, Matt pointed at Diane. 'Our guitarist wrote this one,' he said. Ian hammered out a fragile riff and Matt shadowed it before Diane, her eyes closed, wove a shimmering veil of sound. Matt's voice tore through it:

> *Close my eyes on the face of smoke*
> *Hold the memory in my hand*
> *Long before the world awoke*
> *Echoland*

Diane could smell rotting stone, taste blood in the back of her throat. She bent over her guitar, trying to build a vision from chords. The room suddenly felt cold, as if the walls were open to the night. She'd cut a second finger, and both were bleeding over the metal strings. She looked at the audience. They were utterly still.

> *Close my mouth on the taste of wine*
> *City of bone whose towers stand*
> *Smoky flames in their windows shine*
> *Echoland*

A youth near the front, not someone she knew, was watching her closely. He was thin and had long hair. Diane looked past the audience to the flickering of distant fires in stony windows. It was close enough to touch. But was she seeing or remembering?

> *Slide the needle under my skin*
> *Burned inside me like a brand*
> *The ancient country where dreams begin*
> *Echoland*

After the set, the three musicians downed their rather scrawny rider of Banks' and crisps before hitting the bar. Diane lit a cigarette. Its red glow and wreath of smoke taunted her. A hand touched her arm. It was the thin youth. Close up, he was very pale but had a restless energy. 'Want a drink?' he said.

'Gin. Neat.'

He ordered Bombay Sapphire, a classy touch that she appreciated. They clinked glasses.

'That song of yours,' he said. 'The lost city. I never knew another person had seen it. The black towers. The flames in the windows. I never knew how to get there. But it has to be through another city, like this one. Do you think we could find it together?'

Diane knocked back the blue gin and smiled. 'We could try.' The drink filtered down into her gut, firing the inverted tree of nerve-endings that cradled her unborn vision.

Will lived in Gravelly Hill, near the tangled concrete rune where the expressways met. In the night, she cried out in his arms. He carried on holding her after making love, which held out some kind of promise. Through the faint tides of passing traffic, Diane thought she could hear the lonely music of pipes. The city was no longer dead.

Their relationship outlived the band. Moth fluttered through another dozen gigs, but never made it to a studio. Diane dropped out of university and got a job at the Diskery, a second-hand record shop near the Bull Ring market. She moved into Will's flat, which wasn't really big enough for two, but they weren't leading separate lives. Matt completed his degree and went on to do research on the construction of identity. Ian joined another band; drummers were always a scarce resource.

Will told her he'd first seen Echoland at the age of five. He'd been recovering from the car crash that had killed his parents and nearly cost him his right foot. He still limped in wet weather. 'It's the only thing I remember from that time,' he said. 'And you never see it all the way. Like a double exposure, a world behind this one. Just a hazy outline of black towers and red lights. But it's permanent.'

Diane had been twelve and also in hospital. A clumsily extracted tooth had led to a fever. The episode had coincided for her with the onset of puberty, later than some of her friends. Her strongest memory was a glimpse of a fire blooming in the window of a gaunt black tower. She also remembered a narrow street where veils of grey silk trembled like rain in the arched doorways of houses. That was closer than Will had ever got.

Neither of them was sure where in the world Echoland had belonged. Will thought it was a Mediterranean island – perhaps the one historians thought had been destroyed by a volcanic eruption and renamed Atlantis in western legend. But Diane felt sure it was somewhere colder, more barren, perhaps near Scandinavia. Its secret energy didn't come from the ground, but from some kind of ritual that had taken place there. A ritual the whole of history had been about trying to remember.

Certain places felt close to it: the old viaduct in Digbeth, where narrow roads passed under the black arches; the Vyse Street cemetery with its sealed-up bomb shelters; the derelict factories along the Grand Union Canal. As night fell or day began, these scenes began to reveal their true nature. It was like waiting for the curtain to rise in a theatre. Diane thought Birmingham was a poor cover version of Echoland's forgotten city. Will said all cities were.

Alcohol brought the vision closer as well, but it had a way of taking over. You had to drink fast and then drift as the effects took hold. Strong cider was good for that, with a little vodka to brighten the glow. In the right place, with a few drinks inside her, Diane could feel the heat of the trembling flames, the roses of crimson fire. She could smell the dusty wind, hear music from strange pipes. But she could never step through into the lost country. And after a night like that, another day in the world of traffic and advertisement boards was hardly bearable.

The price of vision was a blind spot where the truth could burn through. Their first summer together passed in a haze of cheap alcohol and weed. A few times they sucked at thin spires of white smoke over tinfoil. The visions left them both unwell, and in September Diane lost her job after turning up late once too often. Will was a freeelance designer, but he was getting less reliable and the contracts weren't getting renewed. Living between two worlds was wearing them down. If they hadn't met Marcus, they might have abandoned the quest.

———

It happened through the Internet, like everything. Will had placed some of Diane's lyrics and poems about the lost country, together with his own artwork, on a MySpace page. He'd always believed that Echoland was a vision all humanity could share, whereas Diane thought it was personal. Among various clueless accolades from New Age dreamers, one had stood out. Marcus not only claimed to have experienced the same elusive glimpses, but had real ideas about how they might break through. Letting someone else into their shared loneliness was a threatening prospect, but there wasn't much choice.

They met him in an anarchist cafe in Alum Rock, on a main road that was clogged with traffic. Like his car, Marcus was small and well-groomed, a decade older than the couple. His smile was the most attractive thing about him. He bought them coffee and cakes, and they shared memories. His visions of the black city in its cradle of barren hills, and the secret fires and woven veils at its heart, had all come in childhood during a long battle with leukaemia. 'Surviving taught me never to give up,' he said. 'I've started a business, made it work, bought a home – but I never got the visions back. I can't do that on my own.'

His plan was for a dedicated campaign. 'Instead of searching for a gateway, we'll build one.' Diane and Will could come regularly to his flat in the jewellery quarter – he'd get a room ready for them to stay in, and together they'd prepare another room as a shrine. 'It's a matter of creating the right ambience. Artwork, music, stuff to take, we'll work on it together. We're the chosen few.'

Marcus gestured towards the window, where car headlights were flickering across the glass. 'They don't have any vision except what's on their TV screens. We're the elite. If we work as a team, we can leave this shithole of a world behind us – and go home. So, are you in?' He looked first at Diane, then at Will. Each of them nodded. Afterwards, Diane wondered why they hadn't looked at each other. They said goodbye to Marcus on the street; he hugged them both, then got in his blue Metro and drove off rapidly. Rain was falling out of the darkness.

As autumn hardened into winter, their lives changed fast. Marcus put them up at his expensive but rather spartan flat in Hockley at the weekends, where the three sampled various drugs and strong drinks. He was convinced that atmosphere made all the difference. 'It's not just getting out of this world, it's finding the right bridge.' He lit red lanterns, put on hypnotic music that was obscure even by Diane's standards. Will didn't want to inject initially, but as he got drawn further into the search it no longer mattered. He was losing interest in the waking world. Marcus usually took less of the stuff than the couple did, which made Diane suspect he regarded them as an experiment; but she supposed someone had to be in control.

She felt that Echoland was nearer than ever – in the hazy waking dreams of long evenings in Marcus' flat, the three of them sprawled on the sofa and carpet, she could feel the secret heat of the window torches, the feather-touch of the drifting grey veils. Nobody was ever in view. She didn't know what the people of Echoland looked like, but from their music she knew they were a sad and gentle race. Maybe the city existed only in the past.

By the end of the year, Diane and Will had moved wholly into Marcus' spare room. He didn't charge them rent, but they did the housework and cooking. The recession had kicked in by then, and neither of them were finding much work. For the time being, Marcus took care of them. But it couldn't go on like that. Matters were accelerating towards a conclusion – whether success or failure, Diane didn't know.

The hardest part for her was coping with all the hangovers and comedowns. It wasn't just Echoland that was denied to her at those times, it was any sense of home and herself. Quite often when she most needed him, Will was unconscious. That was one reason. The other was the way Marcus looked at you while he spoke, as if you were the only person in his world. She didn't trust him, but then the idea of trust was becoming quite threatening to her. So a low-key affair began. Marcus was more forceful than Will, but less demanding. She was sure that Will knew, but he never said anything. In time, she hoped, it would become a true *ménage à trois*. With the three of them sharing a bed. But perhaps they'd have to reach the lost country first.

February was the worst of the winter. Ice melted and refroze, with more dirt in each generation. Diane felt taunted by the weak, infrequent bursts of sunlight. She was caught between worlds, and knew it was her fault. Will was travelling towards the vision, but she couldn't go with him. That hurt her. Marcus was no use: he belonged too much to this world. All three of them were getting ill. They mixed drugs to avoid becoming addicted: hash for a comedown, vodka for withdrawal. After a while, your body felt like a record with so many overdubs you couldn't hear the tune. Sleeping pills joined the other drugs at the table – not for visions, just for getting by. Diane hated looking in the mirror, but she couldn't restore her face blind. She never looked at her body these days. It was swollen with the wrong food, bruised with the wrong sex. If pain was a map of the lost country, why couldn't she find the border for crossing?

The first weekend of March was bright and restless, making Diane put on her little red jacket and go out shopping. The new daylight on the broken old shops – their names and contents mostly changed even in the short time she'd lived here – made her remember how the city had excited her in her teens. When it had reminded her of Echoland. But now, an imitation wouldn't do.

She bought lamb, broccoli and rice. This evening they

could take it easy, maybe watch a film and share a bottle of wine. But when she cooked dinner, Will had no appetite and Marcus was busy on the computer. Diane felt like walking out. But where could she go? How could she possibly reach Echoland on her own? Biting her lip, she took a bottle of Frascati from the fridge and poured half of it into a tumbler, then drank it like water.

The kitchen shelves blurred. The odour of hash smoke drifted from the living room. Diane sat down, refilled the tumbler and closed her eyes. Saw the dark towers falling through a haze of flame and smoke. Ashes flapped towards her; one slipped into her mouth and tasted of nothing. She was sitting at the kitchen table, which was covered with broken glass. Both of her hands were bleeding, torn by splinters. She felt nothing.

A shadow fell over her. Marcus gripped her wrist. 'What happened?'

'Passed out. I don't know. Why didn't you want to eat?'

'Sorry, love. I came to join you.' He brushed a red fragment from her hand. 'Let's get you cleaned up.'

Diane sat numbly while Marcus removed the shattered glass from her skin and the table, then gave her two wads of tissue paper to grip. They reddened slowly as he kissed her.

His fingers began to unbutton her blouse. 'Not here,' Diane said. 'Will might walk in.'

Marcus shook his head. 'He won't be walking anywhere for a little while. But we'd better check he's okay. We left him to his own vices this afternoon. God knows what he took, or how much.'

The only light in the living room was the gas fire. Will had fallen off the sofa, taking a cushion with him, and was lying crooked on the floor like a question mark. Diane switched on the lamp. The cushion under Will's head was soaked with black vomit. He was trembling; under a curtain of straggling hair, his face was glassy with sweat. As Diane reached towards him, Will began to convulse. 'Phone an ambulance!' she cried, trying to hold him still.

'We don't want fucking paramedics in here,' Marcus said. He knelt and gripped Will's legs. 'A few hours' sleep, he'll be okay. Maybe he'll have something to tell us.'

Will's eyes opened, and he tried to speak. Behind him, where the gas fire had been, a gap was opening as if something had burned a hole in the wall. Through it, Diane could see only mist and rubble. She touched Will's face; he didn't stir. Then Marcus was on his feet, pulling at Diane's sleeve, moving towards the ragged opening. A cold wind blew through it, smelling only of dust. Diane gripped Will in her arms and lifted him, dragging his inert body forward. She could hear the faint music of pipes from the other side.

They were in a stone building without windows, but with an unblocked doorway. The chill bit into Diane's face and hands. She'd been right about location; that wasn't much comfort. The weight in her arms pulled her down to the tiled floor, which was littered with stone fragments and pale shreds of fabric. In front of them was a dark stone block with ripples carved into its sides, widening towards its cracked flat top. If it was an altar, there was no sign of any icon. Marcus had gone to the narrow doorway to look out. The corners of the building were blurred with shadow, a part of which detached itself and crept towards Diane and Will as if curious, then retreated. She touched Will's face. He wasn't breathing any more.

Marcus came back, looking confused. 'It's no good,' he said. 'Just ruins.' He sat with his back to the altar, staring at nothing. Diane knelt beside him and pressed her face into his neck. They stayed like that for a while. When she brought her mouth up to his, he didn't see her. Were his lips turning cold, or hers?

Feeling almost too weary to move, Diane stumbled to the doorway. A few crumbling buildings on either side defined a narrow street. There were towers in the distance, but their windows were black. A few fine veils stretched across doorways or between houses, trembling in the wind. There was nobody in sight. Where were the pipers – or was the faint music just the wind in empty buildings?

Diane walked on towards the towers until a hanging veil blocked her path. Drops of moisture glittered in its woven surface. This was the last proof that human presence survived in Echoland. She touched the fabric. It tore, and some of it came away on her hand. The gap reminded her of the portal by which they'd come here. Staring at the silvery net, she saw movement within it: a silent community of tiny spiders.

THIS NIGHT LAST WOMAN

There's a pub in Acocks Green I used to go to regularly. For two reasons. Firstly, there's a lot of middle-aged single women that drink there. Secondly, they have a karaoke night on Saturdays, with a late bar after. I think I'd seen her there a few times before we actually met. I'm not sure. Memories don't stay the same. That's why people need music, to help them remember. And help them feel. If you know what I mean.

It was in October last year. Not long after the terrorist attack on New York. Army shops all over the country had sold out of gas masks. People were scared. Nobody knew what was going to happen. Fortunately, it wasn't the kind of pub where wannabe squaddies went to shout and smash glasses. By Acocks Green standards, it was quite a mixed crowd. That night, a young black guy sang 'Everything I Own' and reduced the whole pub to silence, then a storm of applause. An Irish girl sang 'Zombie', a sadder and much better version than the original.

As usual I was standing near the front, close enough to the bar that I could get a refill every two or three songs. They had an all-night cheap doubles offer. I always like to finish the drink before the ice has melted. To the right of the stage, a group of brightly dressed youngsters were dancing and chatting. Behind me the older crowd, mostly women, were sitting around tables that were already covered with empty glasses. The standard AG types could be seen: young men with heads like light bulbs, women with short jackets and hair tied back hard. Two black security lads were standing just inside the door, keeping an eye out for trouble. I'd been past this place once and everyone was standing outside while five police cars lined up along the road. But that wasn't going to happen tonight.

The white-haired guy running the karaoke machine tried to alternate men and women. With the men, there was a certain kind of song you always got. Three generations of self-pity: Roy Orbison, Neil Diamond, Robbie Williams. The same lonely song, whatever the voice that carried it. The women were more resilient somehow. But as with the booze, it's the cumulative effect that gets to you.

A little fat guy in front of me kept punching the air on the choruses. If he'd had a lighter, he'd have waved it. People were calling for the black lad who'd sung 'Everything I Own', but he'd gone to start a night shift. The karaoke ended with this girl singing 'Fields of Athenry', which I hadn't heard in years. There was something about the idea of a prison ship that made me start crying. I can't explain it.

As the last chords faded, there was a crackle of applause like the static on a poorly tuned radio. I turned back to the bar to get another cheap double vodka. Something tugged at the corner of my eye. A pale face wrapped in shadows. I glanced at her, then looked away. A woman with black hair and a coat the colour of autumn leaves. Her eyes were shining, wet. Someone pushed past me to get to the bar. I felt a kind of vertigo, like there was a darkness around my head.

In front of me, two blokes were talking. *I could change,* one of them said. *There was this night last woman. Made me feel like a different man. The way she was. All gets bright when you're with someone.* I wasn't sure which of them was saying that. Or was it just a voice in my head? I decided to get that drink, but somehow turned back to the dark-haired woman. She was looking straight at me. Her black mascara had run at the corners. We stared at each other for a few seconds.

I'm always nervous about talking to women in pubs. If she brushed me off, I'd have a burning wire in my stomach the rest of the night. But there was something about her, a darkness in her eyes that held me. It felt like we'd already shared something. I crossed over to where she was standing and waited, looking past her at a couple kissing in the shadows. She didn't move away. I looked at her, smiled. Looked at her mouth. She smiled back.

'So you like karaoke too,' I said.

'Yeah. You can't beat those old songs.' She had a Black Country accent. I'd have guessed her age as early thirties. 'Did you hear that black kid earlier? The Ken Boothe song?'

'Yeah, he was brilliant.' I noticed she wasn't holding a glass. 'Want a drink?'

'Vodka and lime. Cheers.'

The disco was starting as I waited at the bar. Madonna, then Gabrielle. We found a couple of seats at the back of the pub, where it was a bit quieter. Her name was Carly. I only caught about half of what she was saying; enough to gather that she lived in Greet and managed a camera shop. She wasn't glamorous, but there was a fragility under the toughness that appealed to me. And she smoked, which I've always found attractive. As we talked, I could feel her breathing smoke onto my face.

'Do you live on your own?' she asked. Her leg was pressed against mine under the table. But when I asked her for a dance, she said no. Near midnight they rang for last orders. As I stumbled to the bar in the half-light, a Judy Boucher song was playing. Couples swayed together, their faces motionless. Earlier, some of the women had been dancing alone; but now, they were either paired up with men or sitting. One of them, hopelessly drunk, threw an arm round me at the bar and ruffled my hair. I shrugged her off and lifted the two drinks by way of explanation.

The lights were so low by then that all I could see of Carly was a ghost of her face, like a paper mask that her cigarette might set on fire. We were talking about our favourite records – a private exchange I won't share with you. It felt like she was a friend as well as someone I might end up fucking. She was a bit on edge, a bit reluctant to open up, but then so was I.

It was a surprisingly warm night for October. She wanted to get a taxi, but I said my flat was only round the block. I needed the walk to clear my head. It was a quiet road full of houses with driveways and security lights. A world away from the Fox Hollies estate on the other side of the pub.

Every time a car drove past, she kissed me to hide her face. I wondered if she was married. Was that one of the things she'd said and I hadn't caught?

'The flat's in a bit of a state,' I mumbled as we reached the block. There was new graffiti on the locked garage doors, but I couldn't read it.

'Don't worry. Whatever it's like, I've seen worse.'

Still, I noticed she was tense as I guided her through the heaps of books and records, and cleared a space on the battered sofa. 'Do you often bring women back here?'

'It's been a while,' I said.

'I was being sarcastic. Don't worry about it.' She sat down without taking her coat off.

'Would you like some coffee?'

Carly looked past me at a bookcase full of flying saucer and conspiracy books. 'Got any booze?'

'What would you like?' As far as I could remember, I had everything. A bit short on mixers, though.

'Vodka'd be nice.' She smiled. Although her face looked tired, her body was like a coiled spring. Maybe another drink would relax her. I needed coffee if we were going to do anything.

But I couldn't pour her a vodka and not have some. The bottle was in the freezer. It stuck to my fingers. I found a couple of shot glasses and washed them carefully.

When I came back into the living room, she'd taken off her coat and shoes. We drank and cuddled for a while, sharing vodka and smoke between our mouths. In spite of the drink, I was getting excited. The loneliness in her called to the loneliness in me. It didn't matter that we were hardly talking.

'Could I have a look at your records?' she said. Most of them were in boxes along the right-hand wall. She knelt there, drink in one hand, flicking through the dusty LPs. I noticed she was shivering.

'Are you cold?' I said. 'I can light the gas fire…'

'No, it's okay.' She stood up and came back to the couch, then reached down and touched my face. 'Let's go to bed,' she said quietly. 'I just have to… where's the bathroom?'

'Through there, second left.' She'd have to pass by the kitchen, but that couldn't be helped. She took her handbag with her. I went through to the bedroom and straightened the duvet, tidied some clothes away in the basket. It should have felt tacky, but it didn't. One-night stands don't have to be cold. It's a chance to be in love for a little while, then let it go. Before the wind blows through the cracks.

When Carly emerged from the bathroom, her eyes were glittering again. 'Are you okay?' I said.

'Yeah. Too much to drink. Could I have a glass of water?'

It took me a while to find another tumbler and wash it. While I was there I poured myself another vodka – a small one, in a shot glass, for later. A nightcap always gives me a sense of security. I took them through into the bedroom. Carly was lying on the duvet, still dressed. She took the glass of water and drank half of it. Her face was a mask. It felt like I'd known her all my life.

We undressed each other slowly. Cars passed by the window, each one lighting up the blind for a few seconds. Her body was taut and muscular. Maybe she went to a gym. She let me turn her on the bed and kiss my way down her spine. Which was when I noticed the scars. They were almost too fine to see, but my lips felt them. Like a white tattoo over her back and legs. A fishing net, for her to flop and writhe in. I wondered how it would feel to walk around in a skin like that. Gently, I turned her round to face me.

The sex took a long time. Partway through, we got under the duvet, where it was warmer. She didn't climax. Women usually don't. When I was spent, she let go of me and lit up a cigarette. I reached for my vodka glass, but my hand shook and I knocked her tumbler off the cabinet. If it had been empty, it wouldn't have broken.

Carly reached down and started gathering the pieces of glass. 'Leave it,' I said. 'I'll tidy it later.'

'How much later?' She lay back on the pillow, breathing smoke. A light gleamed in her left hand: a fragment of glass. 'Give me your hand,' she said.

She held my arm in the air. Slowly, she drew the sharp edge of the glass along it, from the elbow to the wrist. For a few seconds, there was nothing there but a white groove. Then it filled with blood. She drew her tongue along the cut. I couldn't feel much. She looked away. Her face was still again. I lifted the vodka glass with my other hand and drained it.

Then, before I knew it, she was getting dressed. I said nothing. It was cold in the room. I put a tissue on my arm; it stuck there. 'I'd better get home,' she said.

'Would you like me to call a cab?'

'Cheers.' I got dressed, made the call, then took her out into the courtyard. She was still tense, but fighting off sleep. A cat ran in front of us into some bushes, chasing something we hadn't seen. I scribbled down my phone number and passed it to her. A few stars were visible through a gauze of cloud overhead. When the cab arrived, she brushed her lips against mine and muttered, 'See ya.'

69

She didn't phone. I went back to that pub on the next karaoke night, but she wasn't there and I got so drunk I had to leave before I blacked out. I went to the karaoke nights at the Greet Inn and The Village in Moseley, but there was no sign of her. They were shit anyway. Then one evening in November, I was in Alldays buying a pint of milk when I saw her face on the front of the *Evening Mail*.

At first, I thought it was my mind playing tricks. You do that when you miss someone, see them everywhere. Especially as her name was given as Rachael. But unless she had a twin sister, it had to be her. There were more pictures inside. Apparently some guy had picked her up and she'd attacked him with a knife in his flat. He'd fought her off with a telephone, of all things. They'd both ended up in hospital: her with a broken face, him with a badly slashed arm.

But the real story came two days later. It was all over the national papers. She told the police she'd killed three men, only one of whom had already been found. The other two were where she'd said they were: in their city centre flats, stabbed. They'd been there for weeks. The *Mail* said she went for older men without family or friends, because their contacts were harder to trace. The police appealed for anyone who'd seen her to come forward. I kept my mouth shut.

She was in Newbrook Farm Prison by the end of the year. That's in Frankley, on the edge of the Clent Hills. I sent her a card at Christmas, and wrote to the prison requesting permission to visit. The hope of seeing her kept me going through to the new year. I knew she felt as lonely as I did. That was why she hadn't killed me. There was something real between us. She'd been hiding my face, not hers. Yet she'd let me live.

In late January, I got a letter in a long Prison Service envelope. It was from her. Her handwriting was angular and ragged. She said I could come and see her that Sunday at four. It was signed *Carly*. That proved she remembered me. She understood what I'd been through. My anima, my secret soul.

The day I went out to Newbrook Farm was cold and bright. The Clent Hills were crusted with dead bracken. I'd had nothing to drink all day, so I was feeling a bit shaky and sick. It was partly tension. How could I be sure? Pain is a one-way street. I stared at the dark ground and shivered. Her image in my mind kept breaking up into flecks, a newspaper photograph.

The visiting room was a series of glass panes with chairs on either side. You talked through holes in the window. Her face wasn't quite the same. The broken bones hadn't set right. She didn't smile. There was the same tension; confinement hadn't brought her peace. 'How are you keeping?' she asked.

I shrugged. 'Same as ever. How's life here?'

'Not so bad. When you've lived in Tyseley, it all becomes relative.'

'Do they let you listen to music in here?'

'Somehow, I can't be bothered.' Her dark eyes watched me steadily. 'Don't take this the wrong way. But you'll probably never see me outside again.' I nodded. 'So why have you come?'

'I need to know something.' My throat was dry. It felt like the walls around us had disappeared. 'I don't care about what you've done. I need to know... why you didn't kill me.'

There was silence. Twice she began to speak and stopped herself. Then she said quietly: 'Because it wasn't worth it. You're already dying.'

'You don't know that.' I felt the blood rush to my face. 'You don't know. I could break some woman's heart—' She

looked away and laughed. I couldn't hear her laughter through the glass. But I could feel it.

As I left the prison, it was getting dark. The city's lights glowed in the distance, spread below me like a coral reef. From far away, I could hear the voice of a young black man, singing. *You sheltered me from harm.* I waited for the Midland Red bus to Edgbaston. But a local bus came first, and I got on it. I wanted to find a pub where men were playing darts. Where I could brag about my conquests. Have a man-to-man talk about the things that matter. Or just drink.

BIRDS OF PREY

When I was a child, we lived on the second floor of an old-fashioned apartment block that had balconies and railings with black steel roses. Across the road – a long tree-lined avenue – was a park with a small museum at one end. My favourite exhibit was the long glass case of *raptors* or birds of prey. They were perched on branches and rocks or suspended from wires in still flight: eagles, falcons, hawks, buzzards and owls. However long I watched them, I never lost the sense that they would come to life the moment I turned away.

My first year at music college was rather lonely. The other students all seemed to have a lot of money and be very sure of their place in the world. I'd been quite isolated as a teenager, and moving to a small town where I had even more studying to do reinforced that. I used to work through the evenings in my room, then go for nocturnal walks through the narrow backstreets and tree-lined avenues of the student area, blind to any sense of danger.

One night a revving of engines sounded in the distance, like a single machine copied or echoed. Then I could feel a vibration though the pavement. Suddenly motorcycles were gliding past, the stink of their exhaust burning in the night air. The silhouetted image of a dozen or so boys in leather jackets, sitting upright in their saddles, imprinted itself on my vision. Then they were gone.

On Friday nights, I sometimes dropped into the college bar for a pint. One night I saw Robert, another first-year student I'd worked with in violin classes. He was sitting on his own, a hunched silhouette with a crest of dark hair. We said hello and chatted for a while. Unlike me, he was a local boy – 'Never found the way out,' he said. 'Might as well not belong here as anywhere else.'

He asked me what I thought of the music we were studying. 'If you can't give yourself to it, let it speak through you, what's the point?' I made some vacuous comment about the importance of technique. He said: 'Technique is just the vehicle. What drives the vehicle is the spirit in the music.'

Having some company encouraged me to drink more than usual, and I was swaying as we walked out into the narrow street. It was February; our breath left frail scars on the air. A few students cycled past us under the bridge, and I said something about the motorcycle gang I'd seen a few nights before. Robert pulled his coat tighter around his shoulders. 'I used to know them,' he said.

We walked on in silence to the main road, where the pavement glittered with broken glass. Robert told me he was playing a gig at a pub near the college in three nights' time. 'I play the fiddle with a band called Birds of Prey. Come and see us if you like.' His thin hand brushed my arm.

———

The pub had no real stage, just a raised area at the back away from the tables. Birds of Prey turned out to be three music students playing a mixture of what I vaguely recognised as folk and blues standards, with no drums or amplifiers. The singer-guitarist and bass player were sound enough, but Robert's fiddle was what gave the band its edge. He played as if the music was something he had to drive out of his head. It was the same violin I'd heard him play Tchaikovsky on at the college.

In the break after the first set, Robert went to the bar. I suddenly felt nervous about talking to him, as if I might get an electric shock from being too close. Given the age of the sound equipment, that might have been a realistic fear. He saw me on his way back to the band's table, and smiled. I sat holding a glass of strong cider. My hands were trembling.

The second set included a couple of long, fatalistic ballads about betrayal and murder. Robert was playing with his eyes shut, drawn into the chilly world of the songs. The wild energy of the first set didn't return; even the band's instrumental finale was subdued. The audience was getting restless. The end of the gig coincided with last orders, and there was no encore.

As the band were packing up their instruments, I walked up to the stage area and looked at Robert through the wooden railings. His dark hair was out of shape; his face was glossy with sweat. 'That was fantastic,' I said. 'Want a drink?'

'Thanks! Whisky, please. Think we've been better. It's hard when you've been working all day.'

I joined the band at a table where more drinks were already waiting. Robert told me a little about the songs. Most were traditional – from the West Country or the Scottish border – but a few were recent. 'I'll make you a compilation tape,' he said. The singer and bass player exchanged glances. Last orders were renewed, and Robert got another round in.

We left the pub as they were cleaning the tables. Robert was quite drunk; he put his hand on my arm to steady himself. A motorcycle revved up in a nearby street and he glanced around apprehensively. 'Were they here?' he asked.

'Who?' The other two band members had faded away into the mist. The street was nearly empty.

'Doesn't matter.' Robert's face was blank. 'I'm glad you came, Paul. Look, I've got some brandy in my room, would you like to come back for a drink?'

I tried to remember what was happening the next day. 'Sorry, I've got an early lecture tomorrow. Maybe at the weekend, if you like?'

He stared at me for a moment, as if not sure what I'd said. 'That'd be good,' he said. 'I'll make you a tape. See you in college.' His hand reached towards my arm, rose a few inches, fell slowly. 'Take care.'

———

That night, I dreamt I was back in the museum. Wings were beating and claws scraping at the inside of the glass case. Suddenly the front shattered and the air was filled with birds of prey, flying upwards in the dim electric light, circling and swooping. I could see tawny, gold and steel feathers, hard blue eyes, and from something a streak of blood that trailed across the polished floor. I stepped onto broken glass, almost dancing, as hungry birds flapped around my head and sharp talons caught in my hair. The smell in the air wasn't formaldehyde: it was acrid, warm, the mingled scents of feathers and blood.

———————

Despite the electric heater the room was cold; the paper shade trembled from a ceiling draught. The walls were decorated with prints of stark Expressionist paintings. The only light in the room was the red bedside lamp. Robert and I lay side by side on the bed, exploring each other with hands and mouths. Then he slipped over me and I felt his hard penis rubbing against my stomach. I bit his nipples and ran my fingernails down his back. He turned me over, and I gripped the pillow as his arms locked around me and his legs spread inside my own. I felt his fingers applying lubricant, and then his cock thrusting into me. He reached up and ruffled my hair with one hand. Then he was moving inside me, a deep steady rhythm; his bony hands trembled on my shoulders like vestigial wings. I heard him cry out, felt him kiss the back of my neck. He reached under me and stroked me gently until I came over the white cotton sheet. We lay together, kissing in a dazed way, our eyes out of focus, until our breathing returned to normal. Then Robert pulled the duvet over us and we drifted into sleep. I bled afterwards, but not much.

Winter brightened into spring. Robert and I met two or three times a week, usually sleeping together at the weekend, but trying not to look like a couple in public. After all, it was the 1980s and we were only nineteen: anyone could have made trouble for us. I saw him playing with Birds of Prey a few more times that term, and got to know the other two musicians. They both had girlfriends, but seemed glad that Robert had found someone.

Having a lover seemed to take me into a different life: I remember walking home from Robert's bedsit a few times, late at night or early in the morning, and feeling open to every trace of sound or movement – but at the same time strangely invulnerable, as if nothing could touch me. I was also getting used to alcohol, which was already a part of Robert's life. I didn't know then that drink has a jealousy of its own: it always wants you for itself.

As neither of us had a phone in our lodgings, we only spoke when we met. Perhaps that increased my sense of a loneliness in Robert that I couldn't touch. He made love to me as if I was an instrument: something that deserved care and respect, but was still only a way to realise his vision. I used to watch him moving over me, his eyes shut, flying. In some ways I felt closer to him when he was playing the violin. I was a capable musician, a potential teacher perhaps, but I had little of his talent. They never invited me to join the band.

Robert didn't talk much about his past, and I had none to talk about. But one night, after a few drinks, he sat up in bed staring at the curtained window – his head tilted, as if he was listening for something. Cars drove past on the narrow road; in the stillness I could feel their faint vibration, see their lights flicker on the curtains. He turned his head and saw me watching him. A confused smile twisted in his mouth. He looked back at the window and began to speak quietly.

'When I was fifteen there was this boy in my school, Danny. He used to pick on me. Tell other boys I was watching them in the showers, that kind of thing. One time after games he followed me out of school and started asking me questions… what I thought about boys, if I did anything. He persuaded me to go to the reservoir with him and suck him off. It was the first time I'd been with anyone.

'After that, we carried on for more than a year. He left school and started a job, but he used to wait around for me and we'd go somewhere quiet. I let him do what he wanted. Sometimes it was good. But he wouldn't talk to me, wouldn't be seen with me anywhere. And sometimes he was brutal. But I never said no.

'Then Danny started seeing a girl. I didn't see him for a few months. And then, one night, he was waiting for me in an alley near where I lived. He took me to the reservoir again. Made me kneel down, then hit me across the face. He said I'd corrupted him, he couldn't do it with women, if I ever came near him again he'd kill me. Then he knocked me unconscious. When I woke up it was dark. He'd broken three of my ribs, I had to go to hospital. But the first thing I realised when I came round was that he'd come in my face.

'The last time I saw him, he was with some motorcycle gang. They were all speeding down the road together, and I was on the pavement. He swerved to try and hit me. I jumped aside, only just avoided his front wheel. Three years and he's still looking for someone to blame. How much longer?'

I thought about it. 'If you keep on playing the same record, does the tune change?' That made him laugh. I kissed him and we lay down, too tired to do more than hold each other. Robert lay very still, but I knew he was awake. The next day we cycled to a village a few miles out of town, drank cold beer in a sunlit pub garden, then went back through a forest that was bright with growth and warm with decay. Neither of us mentioned what he'd said the night before.

———————

At the end of the spring term, I went home for Easter. Robert came round the night I was packing and gave me a tape that Birds of Prey had just finished recording. I wanted to play it while we were in bed, but Robert asked me to put something else on: 'Don't want to soundtrack my own orgasms.' He left after midnight, and I didn't get to bed until nearly two in the morning. My train was at nine a.m. Still, I could catch up on sleep – and work – when I got home.

I was hardly aware of closing my eyes before we were back in the forest. Robert was running between the trees, trying to dodge the birds that swooped and tore at him from the low branches. Falcons and owls were circling overhead, and a white eagle dropped from the sky to grip Robert's head and smash him into a tree. As he dropped, beaks and talons sprayed his blood over the new leaves. The cries of the raptors were like a motorcycle racing past, fading into the distance.

The room was dark. I rubbed my eyes and tried to focus on the alarm clock. It was half past four. Still confused, I dragged my clothes on and stumbled out of my flat and into the street. If I could warn Robert, maybe it wouldn't happen. There were a few people around: beggars and drunks in their closed orbits, the odd early riser on the way to a morning shift. I ran as fast as I could, but went the wrong way a couple of times and had to retrace my steps. The night sky was overcast, wrapping the town in a cocoon of blurred artificial light.

There was a park quite near the tenement house where Robert lived. We'd walked through it one recent morning, our hangovers exposing us to its poorly maintained state. Running past in the night, I saw a wrecked bicycle caught between some railings. A few yards further on, a figure in a green overcoat was slumped on the ground. Blood was smeared over the pavement around his head. For a moment I let myself imagine his sleep was natural. His hair was clotted with blood, his lips split and bruised. But I could feel his breath on my fingers.

I had to leave him to call an ambulance, but when I came back he was still breathing. While waiting I noticed the muddy tracks on the pavement where narrow wheels had run off the road to trap him. As the ambulance drew into the hospital bay, Robert opened his eyes and looked at me. His lips moved silently. I gripped his hand and he cried out with pain.

An hour later, a nurse told me Robert had been badly knocked about, but he was in no danger; the only fracture was in his right arm. Robert told the police he had no memory of the attack. I didn't catch my train, but the hospital discharged him in the evening and I went home early the next day. Before I left, he told me it was too dangerous to accuse a gang. 'You can stop one, but the rest will get you.'

––––––––––

Robert's arm healed, but his playing was less confident after that. We saw less of each other in the summer term – partly, of course, because we were preparing for the first-year exams. The Bird of Prey gigs were less frequent and more low-key. So was our lovemaking. In the week of exams I felt desperate to be with him, to feel the wings of his desire beating at my back. We finished on the same day, and I left my other fellow-students drinking in the college bar and went to see him.

He was tired, understandably, and didn't return my kiss with his usual hunger. We drank some whisky and dissected the exam papers, agreeing that only a concerted effort by all the lecturers could have been so effective in systematically eradicating fair questions. Then I moved closer to Robert and started to unbutton his shirt. He gently stopped me. 'Paul, I don't feel very well.'

'Then let me make you feel better.' Alcohol, lust and sleep deprivation combined to make me impatient. I brushed his nipple and he gasped with pain. His face was suddenly pale. I waited for him to look at me, but he avoided my eyes. Without quite knowing why I was angry, I gripped his shirt and tore it open, scattering buttons on the faded carpet. His chest and belly were marked with ugly weals and bruises, no more than a day old.

'Robert, what the fuck is...?' I stared at him. 'What's going on?' My mind twisted with sudden rage. 'Who?'

Shivering, he stepped forward and held me against him. Then he put his mouth to my ear and whispered: *Kill me.*

The museum was still pretty much as I remembered it from twelve years before: the dim lighting, the black steel frames around the glass cases. I recognised the Egyptian mummy, the cavern of reptiles, the scorpions in the wall. But the raptors had gone. I walked from end to end of the natural history section, but there was no sign of them and no gap where they might be restored in place. I walked back down the stairs and asked at the reception desk: 'Where are the birds of prey?'

'They haven't been here for years,' the attendant said. 'These exhibits don't last forever. I think they're still in the basement.'

'Can I see them? Please? It's important.'

She thought for a few seconds. 'Are you doing research?' I showed her my college library card. 'Maybe then. I'll ask a colleague.'

Ten minutes later, an older woman led me to the back of the museum and unlocked a door in the wall. She reached up to switch on the light, which made little difference. 'This way.' Our footsteps echoed in the narrow passage. I glimpsed dark shapes on pedestals or hanging from wires on either side.

We went down a flight of steps, along a further passage, then down again to another door, which she pushed open.

Beyond was a dimly lit hall that smelt of formaldehyde and decay. She pointed towards some narrow shapes that I could barely make out. 'Come back when you've found them.' Then she turned and walked back through the doorway, leaving me alone.

The air was cold. As I walked through the hall, I realised the thin standing objects were trees. I felt dead leaves crack beneath my feet. There was a half-moon overhead, and a few stars. I walked on for some time. Then I glimpsed a hawk on a low branch, just above my head. An owl was waiting in the hollow of a trunk. I could just make out a kestrel silhouetted against the midnight blue of the cloudless sky. There was no breath of wind. I stopped.

The raptors gathered around me. They perched on branches, stood on the hard ground, hovered in the air close by. I waited for them to strike. A network of black twigs stood out against the moon. I saw wings outstretched, beaks raised, but no movement. I stripped off my clothes and stood naked.

The birds didn't move. Neither did the moon.

It didn't matter.

THE LAST GALLERY

Even the first time was like a ritual. Buying the razor blades at the local chemist's shop, unwrapping a frail sliver of metal, holding the edge up to the light. Guns were difficult and expensive to buy, and even knives weren't cheap, but this fragment of death cost no more than a postage stamp. The need had been coming on for weeks. Sean had drunk neat vodka for an hour or more, focusing the pain in his mind to a thin streak of light. Then he'd stretched out his left arm on the bare desk and begun to cut.

By midnight, the vodka was gone; the insides of both his arms were slick with blood. Stained tissues were heaped up on the desk like a stage set representing a fire. The real sensation was when he rinsed the cuts under the cold tap: a shudder of pain so pure and delicate an orgasm was dull by comparison. For a few seconds the skin was clean, the wounds dead white. Then the bleeding started again. That was the one part of it he didn't like, the blood.

That was seven years ago. Sean didn't wear T-shirts or go swimming. The only people who saw the marks were his lovers. And he didn't let anyone see fresh cuts, the skin raw and discoloured. After a week they faded to a dull blue-grey, like some cheap building material. After a month they were just pale scars. Some faded altogether, but others formed smooth ridges of scar tissue like Braille.

As time went by, he was less and less sure why he did it. Was it, as a boyfriend had said to him, a way of achieving a sense of control in a chaotic world? Or was it, as a girlfriend had said, a way of punishing himself for imagined crimes? Sometimes he suspected it was a way of pacifying the urge to kill himself that he felt when nothing made sense. At other times he sensed a purpose to it, as if it were some kind of training. Or perhaps, like masturbation, it had no meaning beyond itself.

What Sean didn't believe was the view of one of his radical friends that self-harm was an expression of 'victim culture': a turning inwards towards infantile fantasy, away from the painful challenges of a world in crisis. He knew too many self-harmers: they weren't all narcissistic Goths or fragile neurotics. At the same time, there had to be a reason why so many people were cutting themselves these days. It was like a religion without worship, or a subculture without a name or a uniform. Perhaps there were as many reasons as scars.

There were things that triggered the impulse for him: arguments, failures, sexual rejection, a sense of helplessness. But in the end, they were like the adverts before a film.

When he was alone with a bottle of chilled vodka and a razor blade, nothing else was real. The deep, painful cuts he made in his arms and shoulders weren't a surrogate for anything else. They were the end, in every sense.

Carol worked as a proofreader for the advertising magazine Sean helped to design. They worked different shifts, so it was a while before they got to know each other. The magazine was a weekly catalogue of local goods and services, from lawnmowers to escorts, that was given away through newsagents and hardware stores. The offices were north of the city centre: a district of tower blocks, car parks and expressways, short-lived businesses, people passing through.

Like most office work, it was fairly regimented. No coffees in the first hour; toilet visits kept to a maximum of five minutes; no conversation except during breaks. The hours were long and the pay was dreadful. Most of the people at *City Trade* hoped to move on to a newspaper or a TV station. But if you wanted to work in media, it made sense not to live in Birmingham. It was a city of business: the only message anyone wanted to hear was the marketing message.

Carol was a writer. So far, her only publications were a few short stories in a university magazine called *Present Tense*. Sean played guitar, not very well, and had designed websites for a few local bands. Their creative frustrations sparked a friendship that developed through gigs in shadowy basement bars and maudlin rants fuelled by strong cider. When a company 'right-sizing' process led to most of the work being outsourced, Sean and Carol were among nine people made redundant. After a defiant leaving party at a pub in Newhall Street, they slept together for the first time.

It was a warm night for February, with a hint of rain in the petrol-tinged air. They held hands on the bus, listening to the usual chorus of drunken arguments and stoned freewheeling raps. Sean closed out the voices, but Carol was fascinated. 'I didn't know the bus fare got you a recording contract,' she said. 'It's almost as good as the publishing contract you get for 20p in Snow Hill Station.'

In Sean's tiny flat, they sat on the couch and kissed slowly until the outside world faded away. Carol was a small, muscled woman with a bitterness just below the surface; her mouth tasted of rum and smoke. When he undressed her, he saw that her arms and torso were dotted with cigarette burns – some like tiny crimson rosebuds, others faded to inoculation scars.

'You did that yourself?' he said. She nodded, silently tracing the ridges between his left shoulder and elbow. He kissed her unmarked throat. Too tired and drunk to do much more, they got into bed and caressed each other in the light of the bedside lamp. Traffic went past; a fight broke out in the street. He could feel her breath on his face, but he couldn't hear it. When he woke up, some time after dawn, the lamp was still on. Carol's sleeping face was as still as a mask.

After a mild winter and a spring of feverish rain, the summer had a dull and stagnant feel. Nobody was getting enough sleep. The frequent bomb scares made flights unreliable, while storm damage and flooding made it difficult to travel over land. The newspapers were full of murder and terrorism. The government pledged a crackdown on rap lyrics that encouraged violence or undermined the UK's current wars. The new prime minister had gained the nickname 'Churchill Junior' with such statements as, 'The war on terror will only end when the last terrorist is dead.'

Sean got a job selling low-grade computer accessories in a Yardley shop. Carol was doing office temp work. They saw each other two or three times a week. Carol had made it clear their relationship was exclusive: 'I'm not a timeshare girl.' They both felt the pressure of money worries, and a general sense of failure. They drank too much when they were together, usually going to the off-licence rather than a bar or a restaurant. Sometimes Carol had fresh, angry burns on her skin; sometimes he had thin red cuts like gills. They didn't talk about it.

Once or twice a month, they went to a city centre club called Dream No. 9. It was halfway up John Bright Street, overlooking the expressway. On Friday nights it was a mix of Goths, punks, trannies and assorted weirdos. It was warm on the murky dance floor, and people often took off their tops as the dancing got wilder and sweatier. Some of them had scars, some had tattoos. It was good not to have to cover up. Sean and Carol drank vodka, danced and occasionally necked a few pills there; they separated when they felt like it, but always left together.

One night, Sean was talking with a Lugosi clone at the vodka bar in Dream when he noticed a lot of Goths coming down the stairs together. They looked even more anxious than was normal for them. The barman had just taken a call on his mobile; now he coughed and said loudly: 'We need to leave the building. There's a fire on the top floor. Don't run, but *leave now.*' Carol was on the dance floor up there. Sean wanted to find her, but the staircase was choked with people and there was no way through.

He waited outside, where a hundred or more people in outfits quite ill-suited to the street gazed nervously up at the building. High up on one side, a window broke and smoke belched out. He dug his fingernails into the skin of his left arm, wanting to draw blood. Then Carol was outside the doorway, looking for him. He moved towards her. They kissed and, holding onto each other, stepped back as another window shattered and an angel of flame leered through the gap.

Dream No. 9 was completely destroyed by the fire. No one came to serious harm, though a few people needed treatment for smoke inhalation and a few ankles were sprained. The management claimed the fire had been started by someone smoking in the toilets – smoking heroin presumably, though the speed at which the ruins were demolished and work begun on a new block of private apartments made him wonder in retrospect if that was the truth.

That night, Sean did something he hadn't done before. He got out of the bed where Carol was sleeping, went into the bathroom and cut himself with a fresh razor blade, a dozen or so times. He ran cold water over his left arm for several minutes, until the bleeding slowed. Then he flushed away the bloodstained toilet paper, wrapped some more around his arm and went quietly back to bed.

After that, the last few weeks of summer felt somehow unreal. The sun flared, and the clouds seemed as dense as smoke. There wasn't enough oxygen in the air when the traffic was heavy. In late afternoon, the sunlight was so dense he imagined he could stretch out and float above it, as if the streets were underwater.

One night in September, they went to see a punk band in a pub off St Paul's Square, close to the dark church with its scattering of headstones. As they were leaving, Sean saw a red-haired girl he recognised from Dream No. 9. She smiled at them and slipped a card into his hand, then hurried on to where people were still drinking inside the pub. Carol tucked her head into his shoulder as they walked drunkenly up the hill to Colmore Row. He glanced at the card, remembering that he and Carol had both admired the tracery of scars on the girl's back – though they'd been disturbed by the fact that she couldn't have made them herself.

The card was dark blue, with some words printed in black on one side:

THE LAST GALLERY
37 Trinity Street, B9

It was the coldest day in quite a while. As Sean and Carol walked together through the narrow Digbeth backstreets, rain darkened the pavements and scratched the windows of passing cars. One of Birmingham's oldest industrial districts, Digbeth was trapped in a state of transition: old buildings half-demolished, new buildings half-finished.

Some recent attempts to redevelop the area had stalled when the contractors had decided to pull out in view of the economic climate. The district belonged to Irish pubs, builders' yards and halfway houses.

Trinity Street began close to the viaduct and the railway yards. From the top of the road, you could see three of the viaduct's arches. The lovers walked hand in hand past some empty houses, a boarded-up pub, a church full of scaffolding. This seemed an odd place for an art gallery. Or was it a club of some kind? They might have to come back later, but at least they'd know what to look for.

There were no numbers for a while, then a house was numbered 41. They worked back to 37: a narrow warehouse with an unmarked door and shutters over the windows. It didn't look promising. Sean pressed the buzzer and was surprised, a few seconds later, when the door clicked open. There was a hallway with a side office, a woman who saw them walk in.

Sean held up the card. 'We were given this.'

The receptionist nodded. 'Go through,' she said. 'It's late. You'd better start working immediately.' Sean was about to say that they weren't looking for a job, but it occurred to him that perhaps they were.

The door in front of them opened into a long, high-ceilinged room with some kind of faint blue mercury lighting. It was divided into partitions by wooden or metal frames, hung with some kind of canvas. The air was cool and had a vaguely familiar chemical odour. Sean could see people walking back and forth at the far end of the room, but no one seemed to notice him and Carol. They stood for a few moments, waiting for their eyes to adjust to the thin light, then walked on.

It appeared to be some kind of workshop. The pale canvases on the frames were mostly blank, but a few had been marked with patterns – or with writing in an alphabet Sean didn't recognise. Small tables between the partitions were covered with tools or instruments. Beside him, Carol cried out quietly. She walked up to one of the canvases and touched her fingers against it.

Sean looked at the nearest table. The tools on it were a strange collection: brushes, scalpels, wires, knives, broken glass, something like a tiny sewing machine. As he looked back to the canvas, he realised why the smell was familiar. He'd once worked as a data input assistant at a mortuary. It was formaldehyde.

The canvas was made of skin: a patchwork of different shades, hairless, apparently human. He didn't know if it had come from actual bodies, or been grown through some kind of technology. It didn't matter to him. He took a deep breath of the cool air, and turned back to the table. In a few seconds, he'd found what he needed: a small razor blade set in a wooden handle. Its flawless edge shimmered in the blue light.

Other people would paint, or tattoo, or brand. If this was going to be a record of humanity, there had to be damage as well as art. The skin was where the inner world and the outer world came together. It was dead, but it was full of life. He looked around him at the gallery of skins. Then he stepped forward, biting his lip. Slowly, cautiously at first, he began to cut.

93

MAKING BABIES

That night, she refused to share a bed with him. On the pretext of using the toilet, she went into the baby's room and lay down on the futon they kept for visitors. It was dark, but she could feel the child's eyes on her. His breathing was too shallow for him to be asleep. Half an hour later, Mike came in and shook her. If he couldn't sleep, then she wasn't going to either. Wendy curled into a foetal position and willed herself not to react. Grabbing her left arm with both hands, he pulled her up off the futon. She punched him in the gut. He leant forward, breathing hard, and suddenly released a straight jab that would have broken her face if it had connected. But Wendy had fallen just in time; his fist struck the wall, breaking through plaster to brick. The flesh above two of his knuckles split open like peonies, spraying the wall with blood.

Wendy got up and went to the kitchen for some Band-Aids. Mike remained leaning against the wall, slowly painting it with his burning hand by dragging the wounds against the rough-textured wallpaper. The baby watched through the bars of his cot. *You're the one who keeps us together,* Mike thought.

Neither of them got round to mending or cleaning the wall in the baby's room. Like most forms of damage in the flat, it stayed as a kind of spontaneous art. They lived on the second floor of a reconditioned house, the kind of place you'd rent as a first shared home. But they'd made the mistake of buying it. The house was in Acocks Green, a transition zone between the industrial estates of Tyseley and the yuppie theme park that was Solihull. These forces had warped the district from its placid suburban origins to a kind of tense emptiness, like the hollow inside a guitar. On Sunday mornings, the good mothers and fathers of Acocks Green made their way to the numerous churches on streets that were splashed with vomit and blood.

Late one evening, a couple of weeks after the fight, Wendy caught a bus into town. The man waiting for her was about thirty, with dark curly hair and a gold earring. She recognised him from the photo. They met on the New Street Station concourse, though neither of them had got off a train. 'Shall we go for a drink?' he said. She nodded. They sat together at the back of one of the smoky little pubs off Stephenson Street, discussing work and leisure activities. Neither of them mentioned home life. He worked for a TV repair firm, and spent most of his time driving around South Birmingham. 'The van comes in handy for a lot of things,' he said. But he wasn't as confident as his self-image. People who put ads in the personal columns of the local paper never were. When the duration of their eye contact had increased from a microsecond to the best part of a minute, she touched his arm. 'Let's go.'

His van was parked by the cathedral, a sombre building whose roof-gutters were flecked with starlings like blackfly on a tulip. As she sat beside him, he kissed her. His hands on her shoulders were as tense as mechanical grips. Being an engineer had made her good at dealing with men. 'Would you like to come back to my place?' he said.

Wendy looked at him, then shook her head. 'There isn't time. I know where. Drive up the Warwick Road...' In ten minutes they had reached the part of Tyseley where the railway depot was. There were no houses in sight: only factories and clinics, mostly disused. A local health clinic, opened a year earlier, was now boarded up. 'Stop here.' They got out into a gravel yard by some anonymous three-storey building whose white fluted columns reminded her of a cinema. All its windows were broken. Just beyond it, a segment of canal was decorated with empty bottles and cans. One of the doors to the empty building had been forced open, probably by vagrants. Wendy felt a deep excitement grip her: it was like standing under a railway bridge when a train went past. 'This way.'

Inside the doorway, a short passage led to a surprisingly clean workroom with half a dozen rusty machines that could have been lathes. There was a smell of rotting wood, pungent as unwashed skin. Wendy backed against the wall, pulling her companion with her. The wall made it a kind of threesome. At the end, he collapsed against her as if she'd taken his soul. There was no turning away. She clung to him with genuine tenderness, closing her eyes as he pressed his mouth to the hollow of her throat. The sound of his breath, slowing, timed her descent back to ground level. In the van, he asked: 'How was that?'

'Not bad,' she said. 'My husband's a lot better.' He looked away, then laughed as if he'd decided it was a joke. They drove up to Acocks Green in silence.

He dropped her off at the end of her road, outside a pub where three shaven-headed boys were arguing in the car park. A girl in a black skirt looked on impassively. 'Will I see you again?' he said.

Wendy smiled. 'Of course. I'll phone you soon.' She kissed him deeply, then muttered in his ear: 'But don't hold your breath.' As the van sped away, she looked up into the clear sky: the stars like flaws in black ice. *How did I get like this?* Behind her, the argument became a fight. She hurried away.

In the flat, Mike was watching a video. She walked past him to the baby's room. As usual, the baby was wide awake. His eyes were like china marbles: a deep blue with streaks that were almost black. Wendy hugged him tight. *My poor little angel.* Then Mike was standing behind her. 'Did he turn up?'

'Yes,' she said, putting the child back in his cot. In response to his silence, she added: 'And we did.'

'Any good, was he?'

'Yeah.' She turned to face him, deadpan. 'Much better than you, anyway.'

Mike gripped her arms. 'Tell me what he did. Show me.' She didn't move. He pushed her up against the cot, then turned away and went back to his video. Wendy stood there for a long time in the dark, holding the silent child. Her tears ran down onto her neck, wetting the collar of her blouse, melting the baby's face. The baby's tiny fingers stroked her cheek in mute, uneasy sympathy. *It's all I deserve,* she thought. You couldn't play the game and then expect it to stop because you were hurting. There was no referee. *Except you, my love.*

A week later, she came home from work to find the baby dead. He'd dried up like an orange left in the sun. His fingers had shrivelled and broken off. The black of his pupils had leaked into the whole of both eyes. Wendy felt her throat swelling with grief. The little body hardly weighed anything; she wrapped it in a bath towel, then sat down and waited for Mike to come home. Burial was *his* job.

Three months later, the next was born: a tiny girl whose scalp already bore a few strands of reddish-blonde hair. In a fit of depression, Wendy smashed all the clocks in the flat. She even burned the calendar. 'Time has no meaning,' she explained to Mike. 'Nothing ever changes.' And after the first few weeks of life, the baby didn't really change. All she did was watch and listen. The summer passed by like the heat from a distant fire, felt by someone walking in the night.

On a Sunday evening in late autumn, Mike walked a couple of miles to a block of flats on the edge of Moseley. He picked up a bottle of red wine on the way. Stark trees lined the road, their intricacy revealed by loss of foliage. A rainstorm had marked the pavement with the prints of dead leaves. The light was on in Sarah's third-floor flat. He pressed the button by her number and waited. Her voice on the intercom was flat, like a recording. She didn't say 'Come in', just pressed the buzzer to release the security lock.

Her flat was crowded with dark portraits, wood-carvings, strange fabric designs. They shared the wine, then a joint. Then another. There was no need to talk. Mike felt the room shrinking until there was only him and Sarah and the couch they moved on together. Her arms were a contour map: needle marks camouflaged by fine razor-cuts, a pattern of grooves and ridges. She'd said cutting herself was like sex, only better. You didn't have to come, didn't have to feel anything except what was already in you.

The music broke around them like waves: loud, quiet, loud again. At the end of one track, the singer kept repeating *A denial.* Sarah's dark hair brushed his face like rain. He closed his eyes and watched the sea churning under them in the night. A sudden burst of abrasive guitar playing plunged them into the black depths, exhausted. As his sweat dried, Mike felt cold.

'Why do you stay with Wendy?' she asked when they were dressed again. 'You only seem to hurt each other. Maybe she'd find someone else if she was free. Instead of fucking strangers.' Was it guilt that made Sarah more able to think of Wendy's needs than he was? Or was it because he knew more? *We stay together for the child,* he thought; but he didn't say it.

'We've got things in common,' he said. 'Similar backgrounds, like. Nothing like sharing pain, is there?' He lifted Sarah's hand to his mouth, kissed each fingertip. 'You said you wanted a boyfriend who was more fucked up than you.'

'I know. I'm not bitching. It's just sad, that's all.'

'It used to be sad,' he said. 'Now it's just a tragedy.' Sarah's face hardened, and he knew his smart remark had turned her off. Or brought her down. *Good.* He kissed her cheek and turned to put on his coat. Outside, a cold wind stiffened the trees. Dead leaves cartwheeled across the road like hedgehogs on Ecstasy.

When he got home, Wendy was out. So it was his turn to find the baby dead. He'd been intending to tell her a story, maybe help her to make a picture with bits of coloured paper and fabric. But it was too late now. She'd used her bedding to climb out of the cot, then crawled around the living room until she'd found a pair of scissors. There was blood all over the carpet, slowly turning into rust. She'd stabbed herself in the face a few times before forcing the point of the scissors into her right eye-socket.

The baby's torn skin was already desiccated, papery. *Like a spoilt painting.* He went to the kitchen, got a bowl of hot water and a sponge. But the bloodstains were almost as easy to remove as sunlight. Whatever you tried, nothing could outlive trust. Not for long anyway. Wendy let herself in around three a.m.

Over Christmas, they separated briefly. Wendy stayed with her mother in Wicklow; Mike divided his time between Sarah and some old drinking buddies from his days at the Tech. At the end of December, Wendy came back. Her throat was swollen, and her movements were drowsy and uncoordinated. Mike watched over her, fed her brandy and hot milk, kept the flat warm. Outside, the days were clear and the nights viciously cold: no snow, but a frost that it hurt to touch.

The night before New Year's Eve, Wendy began to struggle for air. Wheezing like an asthmatic, she sat up in bed and wrapped her arms around her knees. Her eyes and mouth were dark holes in a paper mask that was slowly tightening with pain. Nothing happened for several minutes. Then she raised a hand to her throat, which swelled as if she were about to sing. Her mouth opened wide. Then wider still. A tiny white hand emerged from it. Her body shrank into itself, losing definition. The hand was followed by a thin arm, then a shoulder twisted out of shape, then a face.

Wendy huddled on the bed, frozen. The baby, or embryo, struggled free and fell onto the blanket. It turned over, curled up, and lay still. Mike had been watching from the open doorway. He came forward slowly; lack of sleep made black streaks across his vision. *A denial.* He didn't know if their new baby was a boy or a girl, nor how long it would last. But he knew it would be silent. All the children were silent. Their life was a cry.

KEEP THE NIGHT

Maybe he'd drunk too much at the wedding. If everyone around you was getting pissed at the same rate, it was hard to judge. He'd felt a lasting buzz of excitement and happiness for Ray and Susan. Then, later, a growing sense of disappointment in himself for still being single. Later was in the taxi to Euston Station, watching the unfamiliar streets glowing like Polaroids out of the tinted September night. He'd checked the time; no problem. Maybe he'd tried to buy a coffee. All he could remember from Euston was being unable to read the train departure screens. Then falling onto the pale, shiny floor. A ring of white faces around him, staring. That was all.

He woke up on the train, but it felt wrong. The seats were too narrow, and there were no tables. The carriage was too small. Maybe, Alan thought, the last train wasn't always an InterCity one. Did that mean no buffet carriage – no chance to get some coffee and clear his head? It was past midnight. He was prowling the length of the train, which was virtually empty, when they stopped at Tring. He'd never heard of the place. Was this some kind of parallel dimension where empty trains went through the stations of towns that didn't exist? Alan stared at the route map by the carriage door. At least Birmingham was the end of the line. Maybe it was the right train after all.

No buffet carriage. He asked an elderly man in a tweed jacket how far the train went. 'Stops at Milton Keynes,' was the answer. 'No further. Not until morning.' It wasn't good news, though Milton Keynes sounded a little more reassuring than Tring. Alan dug a paperback out of his carrier bag and tried to read, but the alcohol made the sentences run together. Too many words, no meanings. He slowed down and forced the words to make sense. Could he really have blacked out? He remembered a sense of pursuit, of being watched. Maybe someone had helped him get onto the wrong train. At least he'd not been robbed.

As the old man had predicted, the journey terminated at Milton Keynes. It was just gone one a.m. At the ticket barrier, an electronic screen confirmed that the next train to Birmingham was five hours away. The station waiting area was a large square with a few upholstered benches, three potted plants and a cluster of payphones. The far wall was mostly glass, with several doors leading out to a taxi rank. A man with a rucksack was curled up against a concrete pillar, asleep. All the ticket offices were shut. Two brightly dressed young women were sitting by the doors, waiting for a taxi. Alan went up to them and asked if there was a cafe anywhere nearby. 'Well, there's a garage. Does coffee, sandwiches like. About a mile from here. Go left, then right at the first roundabout, then on for a mile or so. It's on the right.' They didn't seem either drunk or tired. He wondered where they'd come from.

Outside, the town centre was shiny and vacant. Nothing was open, apart from a couple of nightclubs on the far side of a car park dusted with broken glass. All the light came from tall, perfectly white streetlamps that resembled toothbrushes. All the roads seemed to be expressways, with minimal pavements and no pedestrian crossings. The first crossroads Alan came to had a large roundabout with some vaguely tree-like structure. He turned right and walked uphill, past some tall buildings that might have been hotels or banks. The promised garage was nowhere in sight, even after twenty minutes' walking. It was cold out here, with so little to trap the heat of people or vehicles. Alan could make out a few clusters of stars in the faintly clouded sky. There was no moon. He wished he'd brought a coat, and some more comfortable shoes.

Eventually he returned to the station where the two young women had gone away. Two teenage couples – the boys in ski jackets, the girls in short cardigans and white skirts – were standing by the telephones arguing about something. He decided not to bother them. Instead, he crossed the empty car park to where a group of security men were guarding the entrance to a nightclub. 'Excuse me,' he said. 'Is there a garage or a cafe or something near here? Anywhere I can get some coffee?' The image of a murky cup of espresso was beginning to appeal to him in an almost sexual way. One of the bouncers gave him directions quite unrelated to those he'd been given earlier. It wasn't like he had anything better to do than follow them.

Half an hour later, Alan turned and headed back towards the station. Route two had been a mirror-image of route one in that it had been equally unsuccessful. He was having trouble finding anything but roads, car parks and giant roundabouts. A few days earlier, he'd seen a TV advert that claimed a new car had been designed by babies. Now he seemed to be spending the night in a town that had been designed by cars. There were no leaves on the pavement. He couldn't believe how quiet it was: no clubgoers, no drunks, no vagrants. The scale and openness of everything, like a school playground. Without the children. After the wedding, it was hard to deal with so much empty space. He'd been at his parents' wedding, but had no memory of it. Unlike their divorce.

With the glass front of the station clearly visible ahead of him, Alan took a detour through a shopping precinct. In a department store window, naked mannequins posed for the streetlamps. Like fashion models that had fallen on hard times. All the shops were new, immaculate and full of darkness. A narrow arcade led him through to another car park, surrounded by what looked like warehouses. Lorries were parked all along one side of it. The tarmac surface was striated with thin yellow lines. From somewhere behind a lorry, maybe the doorway of a building, Alan heard voices arguing. A boy was saying, *Go on, in here. They'll all be round in a minute. You'll have to be ready. Come on.* A girl was saying, *I can't, I can't.* Her voice sounded more irritable and tired than frightened. Alan was surprised by how well their voices carried in the still air. There were no other sounds. He kept walking, back towards the station.

It would be hard to stay awake until the train came; but if he went to sleep, his bag might disappear. One of the two young couples was still waiting by the telephones. The girl looked cold; unlike her boyfriend, she didn't have a jacket. An inch of white skin was visible above her waist. From where Alan sat, he could hear them whispering but couldn't make out the words. Then one of the phones rang, and the boy answered it. There was a brief, muttered exchange. To disguise his curiosity, Alan fished the paperback out of his carrier bag and started reading. The boy hung up the phone and embraced the girl, silently. He was much taller than her. They backed into a shadowy alcove behind the telephones and stood there, pressed together, hardly moving.

A while later, the other couple returned. The four of them sat by the telephones, waiting for one to ring. When it did, the couple who'd been together in the alcove left to get a taxi. Then the two girls whom Alan had spoken to earlier came back and sat by the glass wall. None of them could be older than eighteen. Alan felt a mixture of sadness and excitement. This was what it came down to, he thought. Take away the bedroom, but keep the night. The saddest thing was how they seemed to be looking after each other. How quiet and vulnerable they were. He wondered if the boys were for sale too, or if they were running things. Not that Alan was interested. He felt bad enough, just being a witness.

Unable to concentrate on the book, he wandered down to the nearest platform. It was empty. The digital clock display clacked loudly as its numbered slats moved. In the Gents' toilet, the only mirror was a polished metal sheet that blurred and stained his face. He felt like an image, trapped

107

between the night inside him and the night around him. The urinals were bright ovals of steel, hoods without faces. He thought of the young couple in the alcove: the girl's white legs tense with cold.

Back in the waiting area, the two girls had gone off again. A young Rastafarian bloke was sitting where Alan had been. 'Waiting for the London train, mate?'

Alan shook his head. 'Birmingham.' It was still a couple of hours off. 'You're from London?'

'Edgware. Got a job up here. Bit of a dead place, though. Know what I mean? Wouldn't like to live here.' He shivered. A telephone rang and a boy answered it. 'Got a newspaper?' Alan shook his head. 'Can I borrow your book?' Alan realised the paperback was sitting in his hands, unopened. He shrugged and passed it over. It was Derek Raymond's last novel. The youth read the first few pages intently, chewing his lip. Then he looked at Alan, his expression a mixture of disgust and confusion, and passed the book back to him. Alan felt viciously amused, then cheap. He'd forgotten how moral Rastafarians tended to be, despite his North Birmingham upbringing. He considered apologising, but couldn't make the effort. Twenty minutes later, the youth stood up and stretched, his rucksack jumping on his shoulders like a child. 'My train's due. See you, mate. Safe journey.'

Outside, the first light of dawn was beginning to rise off the concrete surfaces like mist. It seemed cooler than before. Alan closed his eyes and drifted into uneasy sleep, too light for dreaming. He was woken by the sound of boots on the hard floor. A small bearded man in a uniform was pushing a trolley up to the ticket barrier. The teenagers were gone.

Alan stood up and felt dizziness close a fist around his head. Time for a short walk, before the train.

The streets were bare. A metal-panelled office building shimmered faintly, unable to reflect more than light. He couldn't imagine people walking around here. This town centre went on forever. He walked slowly, fatigue dragging at his ankles. The sky was a clouded pane of glass. It wouldn't let the light through. He cut through an alleyway between two warehouse-type buildings. A car park, laid with black gravel, criss-crossed with bollards to discourage joyriding. Alan stopped. He didn't know what he wanted. Forget it. The train would take him out of here. Then a hand touched his sleeve. 'You.'

It was the girl from the station. The one with the tall boyfriend. He was standing behind her. 'Come with us,' she said. They walked on through the car park, without looking back. Alan bit his lip. The telephones. He took a deep breath and started after them. They still looked like a couple, walking in step, not quite touching. The cold made his fingers numb. Only the changing view told him he was still walking. On the far side of the car park, he followed them into an alley littered with chip papers and salmon-pink condoms. Beyond that, two kebab vans were parked outside a nightclub. Empty bottles, wrappers and drying scabs of vomit indicated a nocturnal crowd. How did they get home from here?

A footbridge led over a car park, roofs gleaming like stepping-stones on the pale gravel. And then, at last, some trees. Their leaves were black in the weak dawn light. Their branches twisted around each other, as if they were drunks leaning together. In the middle of this unreal-looking crescent of trees was a fixed caravan. Alan was surprised it hadn't been towed away. The young couple stopped. The girl turned towards Alan. 'In here. Thirty quid.' She stared at him until he reached into his pocket for the money.

Inside were a small kitchen and a living room, most of which was taken up by a double mattress. There were a few plastic chairs with people sitting on them. More people were standing in the corners and doorways, all facing inwards. The windows had some patterned fabric nailed over them. The only light was a naked red bulb in a floor lamp, near the mattress. It was warm in here: the trapped heat of a dozen or so bodies. Without hesitating, Alan found a bit of floor space and sat down among the audience. He couldn't see what kind of people they were. It didn't matter. The boy and the girl kicked off their shoes and knelt together on the mattress, which was stained with dried sweat and blood. For a moment, the light creased.

The couple stripped down to their underwear. Then the boy picked up the girl's flimsy vest and ripped it down the middle. 'You only do this to hurt me,' he said. 'To torment me.' The quiet rage in his voice made Alan's throat tighten. He could feel sweat prickling his shoulder blades. 'Fuck you.' The boy reached out, touched the girl's throat. 'That's a love-bite. Who did that to you?'

'I'm sick of this.' She gripped his hand, digging her nails into his skin. He stared at the tiny wounds, the dark blood growing in them. 'You're ill. The things you told me. No wonder I can't bear—' His first blow made her face jerk back like a puppet. The blood on the back of his hand smeared across her cheek. 'How much longer have I got to live inside your madness?'

He smacked the side of her face, then gripped her hair and tugged. Her scream was as much fury as pain. She fell heavily across the mattress. He knelt between her legs, his fists clenched. When she tried to get up, he pulled at her knickers. She stumbled over him, drew back a foot and kicked him hard in the crotch. He curled up on the floor, screaming and weeping. She reached behind the lamp, raised something to her face. It was a framed photograph. She smashed it into her own forehead. A fringe of blood dripped across her eyes. The boy ground his face into the carpet, almost choking on his own screams. Their voices were indistinguishable now.

The watchers were so still, they didn't seem to be breathing. Only their eyes moved: glancing from one figure to another, then back to the stained mattress between them. Alan forced himself to look away from the scene, at the people around him. Their eyes were huge and swollen with light. Too big for human eyes, or a human conscience. He wondered how any skull could hold them. But even that wasn't enough to make him stand up and walk out of the caravan. What did it was the boy's tired voice, rising like smoke from the dirty floor. 'One more night like this, and I swear. I swear, I'll kill you.'

Alan stumbled back across the footbridge, not bothering to wipe the tears from his cooling face. He'd left the caravan door open. How many performances had those terrible wide-eyed voyeurs – or witnesses – paid to see? How many times had that couple gone through their routine? *Jesus Christ. Thirty quid.* So little money. Anything could be deregulated now. There was even a market for these offcuts of the soul. As the morning brightened around him, Alan

111

ran and wept and struggled for breath. The images of the fighting couple, trapped in the death-agony of what united them, peeled slowly from his memory. But the audience wouldn't go. Sitting or standing there, crowded together but not touching. Like photographic negatives, unable to change or look away.

He'd missed his train, but the next one was less than half an hour away now. Men in uniform were opening up the ticket offices and untying bundles of newspapers for the kiosk. Alan blinked at the waiting area. It seemed duller and shabbier by daylight. He walked through the ticket barrier into the tunnel that led to the platforms. Something caught between his feet and almost sent him flying. He looked down. It was a telephone receiver, trailing a few inches of severed flex. Catching his breath, he walked on down the metal steps to Platform 3. The clack of moving slats made time painful; but the tracks merged in a circle of daylight that was tinged with pink and gold, like something alive. Ten minutes ahead of time, the tunnel shuddered and the train came in. It was almost empty of passengers. He felt a kind of quiet calm pass through him, an acceptance of the world.

MY VOICE IS DEAD

We are the sacred body of Christ, not some bunch of secular do-gooders.
– anonymous Internet posting

The name rang a bell, but Stephen wasn't sure where he'd seen it. Maybe in his student days, when insomnia and random second-hand books had taken him down some strange roads. But he'd been curious, not gullible, and this looked suspiciously like a cult. A mythical realm with dark towers, a ghostly lake, and a king in tattered clothes like some iconic hobo? Surely even in his mixed-up youth, he couldn't have confused faith with a bad dream like that? But something about the feverish words drew him in, made him keep opening the page. Perhaps its sheer morbidity appealed to him now that he was, objectively speaking, close to death.

The anonymous creator of the Yellow Sign website used some dense, archaic font that resembled medieval script. His long paragraphs were interspersed with amateurish sketches and blurred photos meant to illustrate the text, for all the world as if he were a travel writer rather than a delusional fantasist. A black-and-white photo of a derelict industrial landscape, with two crumbling brick towers, was captioned *The ruined city of Carcosa*. Another photo appeared to show the edge of a lake whose water looked almost black, and was completely still though the clouds overhead were in turmoil. That was captioned *The lake of Hali in permanent twilight*. Of course, Stephen reflected, that probably wasn't meant to be taken literally.

Then there were a few crude drawings, possibly made with charcoal and scanned into the page, of crippled birds and misshapen human figures that lurked around the lake and the ruined buildings. And the Yellow Sign itself, an asymmetrical logo incorporated into every photo and sketch as if hanging in the air wherever you might look. When Stephen closed his eyes it shimmered there, an unhealthy shade of yellow he'd never seen in real life.

At the end, there was an e-mail address for anyone who wanted to know more. Stephen clicked on it and typed a short message: *I don't know where Carcosa is, but it's got to be a better place than where I am. Will you go waltzing Cassilda with me? A realm of eternal twilight would beat this world where they switch on stage lights and call it day. Tell me where to find Carcosa. I don't have long. Hastur la vista, baby.*

After sending the message, he turned off his computer and tried to pray. But the words wouldn't come. Was God shutting him out for dabbling in a bit of arty folk-religion?

I didn't mean it, he thought, crossing himself. Then he took the rosary from his bedside cabinet and counted the beads steadily until his panic subsided. After the surgery and chemotherapy, he'd been declared free of tumours and told to go back for routine monthly checks. The last of which had revealed a sudden rise in tumour marker levels, calling for an MRI scan. In three days' time he'd know the results. Surely he could be forgiven for clutching at a few straws.

Of course, all this Ryan Report business wasn't helping. He'd read the coverage in the *Irish Times* with a mixture of rage and shame. Rage at the feeding frenzy that was taking place in the Protestant media, but also at the sheer foolishness of the Church authorities who'd tried to cover up what they should have stamped out. If co-operating with the police was too dangerous, they should have made sure a few of the offenders met with nasty accidents. After all, whatever the papers said, there weren't many of them.

And shame at what might have taken place if the accusations were true, if it wasn't just a bunch of lowlifes blaming their carers and educators for the fact that their lives had come to nothing. Whenever he thought about the alleged crimes, other thoughts got in the way: the fact that those brats would have starved or turned to crime without the care and support the Church offered. He literally couldn't imagine what they said had happened. But not having words for the shame – being slightly ashamed of experiencing it, even – didn't make it go away.

His hands were trembling as he returned the rosary to its drawer. It was nearly midday and he'd got nothing done. In the past, he'd have filled a day off with activity: gone somewhere outside Birmingham, or done some reading at the library, or assembled a new bookcase. But now he didn't have the energy, and it was hard to see the point. When his usual routine lapsed, there was nothing there. Stephen wondered if the pain in his back was anything more than the effect of sitting still too long. Suddenly angry, he marched into the kitchen and started wiping the surfaces, washing up a few mugs, then reaching up to wipe a cobweb from the window. How long had it been there? He strode through the house with a duster, rubbing at shelves and pictures. The computer screen was dusty too but he didn't want to touch it, the machine didn't deserve his attention. He reached to switch it back on, then turned away and went back to the kitchen. There he sat at the table, clasped his hands and pressed them to his forehead, weeping. It wasn't much of a prayer, but it was something.

––––––––––

The bright February light skittered off windows and pools of rainwater. Stephen locked the front door and walked through into his front room, the room he always kept tidy and clean, the room for entertaining visitors (what with, his puns?). Its order and familiarity always calmed him, but not now. He waited to feel at home. Inoperable. Behind that word lay more closure than Woolworth's. Oddly, he didn't really feel ill. Just tired.

The computer called him and he resisted just long enough to pour himself a glass of Jameson's. There were only two new e-mails, both with the title 'The exile returns'. Which was a sure sign of spam. But one of them was from his sister Claire. The other was from 'Death in Jaune'.

Claire's e-mail said she hoped he was okay. Then there was a link to the local paper's website, with the comment: *This man married me and Ian. I feel betrayed.*

Breathing deeply, aware of a faint stiffness in his lungs, Stephen clicked on the link. A face he recognised from somewhere. Richard Robinson, aged seventy-three, had been jailed for twenty-one years by Birmingham Crown Court for multiple rapes of children. A former local priest, known for his motorcycle and friendly manner, he'd quit the country in 1983 to escape prosecution. It had taken the police a quarter of a century to extradite him. All along, the article said, the Church had kept his whereabouts a secret. Up to 2001, they had continued to pay him a regular salary.

Sentencing Robinson to spend the rest of his life in prison, the judge had called for an inquiry into the Church's actions. Stephen noticed his glass was empty but he didn't remember drinking, couldn't taste the whisky or feel it in his chest.

He felt more helpless now than he had at the hospital. Father Robinson. He remembered that smiling face at Claire's wedding and other times. Remembered, now, them saying he'd left the priesthood. Scrolling down the long list of comments, he saw nothing but the cheapness of Protestant minds. As if the Church had no higher purpose than trawling through the mire of dubious accusations and worthless lives. One earnest local had declared: *For any priest to go on spouting Latin before the faithful when his church is guilty of such crimes is a vile hypocrisy.*

That was enough. His fingers trembled as he clicked into the empty comment box and typed: *We are the sacred body of Christ, not some bunch of secular do-gooders.* Then he turned from the computer and crossed to his study window. Tiny flakes of sleet were blowing against the glass like dead skin. He ought to phone Claire, she'd sounded upset. No, he'd reply to her e-mail. That way, he wouldn't have to burden her with his own bad news.

The faint hum of the computer was soothing, like the gentle undertow of painkillers. Stephen opened the other 'The exile returns' message. It was in the same archaic font as the Yellow Sign website:

> *O pilgrim of Carcosa grim*
> *Our voices share a common hymn*
> *The Lake of Hali holds the word*
> *Forgotten by the mindless herd*
>
> *The King exists! He has returned*
> *To where the black stars ever burned*
> *And in his sacred yellow cloak*
> *He proves that God is not a joke*
>
> *Cassilda dances like a rune*
> *Beneath a different kind of moon*
> *If for true vision you would ask*
> *Then gaze upon her pallid mask*
>
> *This is long over, and to come*
> *The stones cry out, the mouth is dumb*
> *The King in Yellow – read the text*
> *And then remember what comes next*

Underneath the verses was another blurred Polaroid

photograph: the statue of a woman lying in a white casket, her thin arms crossed over her chest. Her face was a flawless marble cast. The eyes, lips and nostrils were sealed. It reminded Stephen of a carving on the tomb of a saint. The pure spirituality of it took his breath away. Behind the figure, cinders from a hidden fire were rising through bare trees.

That weekend, he found a copy of *The King in Yellow* in Reader's World, the only second-hand bookshop remaining in the city. The paperback had no date. Inside, there was a reproduction of the original cover from 1895: a cloaked man standing before a runic sign, with a cyclone twisted around him. Pain struck him on the bus, left him almost helpless, but just managing not to vomit. He got off near his home and collapsed onto a bench, curled up like a foetus. Nobody offered to help him. Finally he managed to stumble back to his flat, the book in his coat pocket. The evening was so bad he nearly called an ambulance. But around two in the morning, the pain and nausea subsided. The peace was too valuable to waste on sleep, so he reached for the book and started reading.

It was a book about a book that didn't exist: a play that had been published but never performed. The narrator of the first story was a bigoted Catholic who hated Jews and clearly disliked women. He turned out to be a violent psychopath driven mad by the play. What was the point of that? The second story was a weird nightmare about people turning to stone and then coming back to life. Much better. The third story plunged back into the twisted world of the play, which seemed to offer a morbid spiritual realm of its own. And then the fourth story, 'The Yellow Sign'. He'd never read anything so disturbing. A more sympathetic Catholic narrator – whose only crime was wasting the chance to make love to his girlfriend. She gave him a carved symbol and then was killed by a rotting man who had come to take it back. The narrator ended up dying, alone, in terror and confusion.

If he'd read the stories before, however long ago, surely he'd remember. They would have troubled him at the time. If not, why did they seem so familiar? What did they remind him of?

Stephen didn't sleep that night. By now he was signed off work, living very much one day at a time. Soon it would be the hospital, and then maybe a hospice. He might have six months, but what kind of months would they be? How long would he be waiting for a Yellow Sign to release him into the dark? And for which sins was he now being punished? He rather wished he'd tried a few more interesting ones. It was too late now. Flesh and pleasure didn't mix any more.

A week after reading the book, he e-mailed his nameless correspondent: *If Carcosa is real, tell me where it is. I don't have much time. A few more weeks or months of walking and thinking. Then however long doing nothing but dying. If the King can give me hope, I'll do anything.* Before he pressed 'send', he wrenched the silver cross from its chain around his neck and dropped it on the carpet.

The answer came back an hour later: *O pilgrim, do not despair. Carcosa is permanent. I have been here for a hundred years or more. Carcosa endures because it makes itself part of death, which the world cannot. The King is in tatters, the Lake of Hali is in twilight, the Pallid Mask never changes. Life fades but death goes on forever. I think you are ready to join us. Bring what money you have, but send nothing. Go by train to Telford, where Cassilda will meet you with a kiss, tomorrow at noon.*

The train was late; he was afraid she would have gone. A cold wind was blowing across the platform. Clutching a weekend bag, he looked around. A young woman came out of the waiting room and headed towards him. She didn't match his mental image of Cassilda: her dark hair was too short, her clothes too modern. But what was he supposed to expect? Then her eyes met his and she smiled as if waking from an erotic dream. Without asking his name, she gripped his free hand and kissed him on the mouth. It was more of a kiss than he expected or deserved, and he was surprised to feel himself respond. It had been a long time.

Still holding his hand, she led him down the concrete steps to the car park. A man was waiting in a rusty blue Metro. Cassilda opened the back doors and got in beside Stephen. 'Welcome to Carcosa,' the driver said, starting the engine. He was thirty or so, with a checked shirt and pale cropped hair. The car turned away from the town, heading out between mist-wreathed fields. Cassilda leant back into Stephen's arms and raised her mouth towards his. He'd heard that cults did this, used sex to win new converts. But frankly, what did he have to lose?

As the road narrowed and the fields gave way to the bones of a forest, Stephen began to slip back in the cold undertow of pain and nausea. He reached in his bag for medication, gulped two different pills. Cassilda gestured towards her mouth. 'It's medicine,' he said. She shrugged. The driver was watching them in his mirror. On the dark trees, streaks of mould flickered like discoloured runes.

'Are we going to the lake?' Stephen asked. Cassilda nodded slowly. 'How long have you lived there?'

The young man answered: 'There is no time in Carcosa. The moon never changes.'

'I've been here three months,' Cassilda said in a soft Derbyshire accent. 'Hastur's just jealous because he only joined us last week.' She gave Stephen a conspiratorial smile and rested her head on his shoulder.

They drove on in silence. The forest thinned out at the edge of a derelict estate, identical grey blocks with sheets of metal nailed over their windows. A teenage couple with a pram crossed the narrow road in front of the car. The driver pressed on his horn. 'Mindless creatures,' he muttered. 'If I ran them down, who'd know the difference? Their world means less than the world of slugs. You haven't told anyone where you're going, have you?'

'Course not,' Stephen replied. The question made him realise he should phone Claire at least, let her know he'd gone away. If there were phones wherever they were taking him. He didn't have a mobile.

The air seemed to thicken, like smoke with a flickering yellow flame somewhere behind it. Were his eyes giving way? The buildings were shapeless and blurred. It was too early for twilight. A crow larger than any he'd seen before, its plumage streaked with white, flapped unsteadily above the road. Then, suddenly, they passed a ridge and were heading downhill towards a lake whose surface was a metallic blue-grey. On either side was a burnt-out tower block. 'We are lost in Carcosa,' the girl said, so faintly he wasn't sure he'd really heard the words. The car shuddered to a halt where the road approached the stony lakeside. As Stephen opened the door, a stench of decay struck him. The clouds overhead were bruised with turbulence. Something brushed his face like an invisible wing, and sickness gripped his bowels. The other two walked on as he crouched by the roadside and vomited. Metallic runes flickered above the dark water.

Looking up with tears in his eyes, he saw a twisted shape flapping towards him over the water, like a yellowish cloak with nothing inside it but with purposeful movement. He rubbed his eyes and the shape faded – but now he could make out smaller buildings on the far side of the lake, and people moving between them. A dozen or so prefab huts, and a thin white building with a steeple. There was something attached to the steeple, but from this side he couldn't see what it was – only the framework of boards and scaffolding that held it in place. Then, just at the point when the hallucinatory cloak would have reached him, pain gripped his lower spine and the world became grey. The waters of the lake were churning slowly. The last thing he was aware of was the taste of blood in his mouth.

'Drink this.' The man leaning over him was himself. Stephen took the offered glass of tawny liquid and swallowed. It was cognac, a delicate flame in his mouth. His body remembered the pain and he swallowed again, then a third time. The man took his empty glass. It wasn't his double,

Stephen realised, though the resemblance was striking: a balding man in his fifties, with a narrow face and steel-framed glasses. The fire was spreading to his throat and chest. He was lying on a narrow bed, in a tiny room with plasterboard walls and an electric fan heater. Another man was standing beside the head of the bed, looking down: the driver.

'Don't worry,' the older man said. 'You're in Carcosa. We can save you. When you can stand up, we'll take you to the King. And at sunset, he will perform the ceremony of the Pallid Mask.'

'Is he an Elvis impersonator?' Stephen asked.

Hastur twitched angrily, but the older man smiled. 'No, Elvis was an impersonator of him. I've read your messages, I know you're in trouble. But we're prepared.'

Stephen closed his eyes and pressed his hands together, as if praying. But in this place he didn't know the words. His fingers brushed his dry lips. 'Is Cassilda here?' he said. Neither man answered. He opened his eyes. 'All right.'

'Do you have money?' Hastur said. Stephen reached for his wallet and handed it over silently. It contained four hundred pounds, all he could take out before his next salary payment.

They left the hut, the older man supporting Stephen and Hastur walking behind. They were close to the edge of the lake, which stirred restlessly. Dense clouds of blue-green algae hung beneath its dull surface. The air seemed denser than before, harder to breathe, and the clouds held motionless flakes of darkness.

From this side, he could see that the white building held up a twisted yellow shape, a rune or abstract design he remembered from the website. It was hard to look away, but his guide was leading him to a caravan parked opposite the chapel. Hastur knocked three times and waited.

The door opened. 'Come in,' said the King. He was a tall, slightly hunched man wrapped from head to foot in a ragged cloak. Stephen thought it was made from pieces of other clothes – an army uniform, a priest's vestment, a surgeon's gown, a business suit – crudely stitched together and dyed or sprayed with a vivid yellow pigment. He must be wearing something black underneath, since the tears in the fabric revealed only darkness.

The interior of the caravan stank of incense and alcohol. Its walls were papered with newspaper stories, but in the dim light of two candles he couldn't read the headlines. The table was covered with books, newspapers, empty bottles and other objects. There were only two chairs; the King gestured to Stephen to take one, then sat down facing him. The other two men remained standing.

'Welcome to Carcosa,' the King said. He filled two shot glasses from an open bottle and passed one to Stephen. 'Tonight you will see the Pallid Mask. You will hear the Hyades sing. And as the black stars shine over the lake of Hali, you will be redeemed. And you will dwell among us forever.'

The other two men chanted something in a language Stephen didn't know. The King raised his glass and drank, and Stephen followed suit. The drink was also new to him: a spirit that tasted faintly of smoke and decay. It numbed his mouth and filtered through his gut like a wave of stillness. Within seconds, the world seemed clear and without pain. He gazed through tears of relief at the King's narrow, immobile face.

'Bring me the Pallid Mask,' the King said. Hastur stepped through into a back room and returned with a small leather suitcase, which the King placed on the table and unlocked. It contained two objects wrapped in yellow cloth. The King carefully unwrapped the larger bundle. His fingers were thin and very pale. He held up the mask and passed it to Stephen. 'Feel the weight of it.'

The mask was not plaster. It was carved from marble or quartz, with crystals twinkling in its pure white surface. A young woman's face, with perfect features; the eyes and mouth were shut, the nostrils filled in. Stephen's hands were barely strong enough to lift it. Around the edge were a number of small holes, crusted with dried blood.

He passed it back to the King, who had already opened the second bundle: an electric screwdriver and a plastic box of screws. The King refastened the bundles and passed one to each of his acolytes. Then he looked across the crowded table at Stephen, holding his eyes for a long moment. 'The world is poisoned,' he said. 'Nothing of value remains. Time to go.'

———

The sun was setting as they waited outside the chapel. More people came from the huts and the ruined towers. They were all cheaply dressed and looked sick or troubled, but given strength by a shared expectation. The algae blooming in the dead lake seethed with a mysterious energy. The air was close to freezing point.

Three slender figures emerged from one of the nearest huts: teenage girls, possibly sisters, dressed in long coats. They glanced anxiously at the King, who tapped his watch. 'Sorry,' one of them said. 'We were practising.' Stephen wondered if they were the Hyades. The King walked up the steps to the chapel door and took out a large key, then waited.

Finally, three more people joined the congregation: two men flanking a young woman, who appeared to be heavily drugged. Despite the chill she was wearing a sleeveless white gown. As they slowly approached the chapel, he realised the girl was Cassilda. Her eyes tracked across the congregation, from face to face; he looked away. Her minders helped her climb the stone steps to the chapel door. At that moment, the sun's last rays caught the Yellow Sign and made it writhe.

The King twisted the key and pushed open the heavy door. Cassilda's guards took her through the doorway after him. The Yellow Sign faded with the daylight; black waves crashed on the lake shore. One by one, the people of Carcosa stepped into the chapel.

A HAIRLINE CRACK

They hadn't spoken since the train had left Richmond. Gary was browsing through a copy of the *Sunday Times* that someone else had left on the table, occasionally muttering to himself about New Labour out-fascisting the Murdoch press. Alan was lost in the view through the sweaty train window, where rain streamed down a landscape of willows and poplars. It was like a blurred Impressionist painting without the colour. They were on their way to visit Gary's parents; maybe that was why Alan was being so difficult about everything. However, Gary suspected that there was an underlying reason that had to do with Alan being a cunt.

As the train slowed down and stopped at Guildford, Alan seemed to wake up. He pressed his face against the thick glass and stared, then rose as if meaning to open the window. The windows on these trains didn't open. He sat back down again, slowly. As the train started up again,

Gary watched a cluster of blank faces turn away from it. A young man in a tweed jacket two generations too old for him sat down at the next table, pulled out a mobile phone the size of a playing card and began shouting: 'Jed? Darren here. Listen, we've got to get this ad campaign sorted. Time is money. Minutes is megabucks. How are we going to slant this?'

'Did you see that kid?' Alan muttered.

'What kid? Where?' He didn't give a flying toss, but it was better to pretend interest. Otherwise, he'd get the silent treatment all week.

'On the platform. There was a boy. Seventeen, maybe eighteen. Had this fringe that covered his eyes completely. Black hair. Fringe down to the end of his nose, I'm not kidding.'

'I'm not caring. Your teenager fixation is entirely your own problem.'

'Where's the problem?' Alan had that rapt, Duchovny look again. 'With a fringe that long, I wonder how he sees where he's going.'

'He probably doesn't. He probably just walks through the same blind, sleepwalking routine as the rest of us.'

Alan looked back at the window. The rain was a translucent sheet, a car wash. Hazy trees jittered in the cloud-formed twilight. Gary felt slightly sick. Another hour on the train, then a long walk through what was probably going to be a river across Worthing. And Alan in lech mode yet again. Why the fuck did he put up with it?

During a long stretch of repetitive, overcast countryside, Alan suddenly looked up and said: 'You know that boy I mentioned?'

Gary spontaneously ripped the *Times* leader column in half. 'Will you shut the fuck up about that boy?' he snarled. The young fogey at the next table almost dropped his mobile phone.

'No,' Alan said. 'You don't understand.' Gary paused, wondering whether that phone might be large enough to have a future as Exhibit A. In Alan's case, probably not. 'It's not the boy,' he said, a weird expression on his thin face. 'It's the fringe.'

'Just because you're going bald, sweetness, is no reason to obsess over—'

'You don't get it, do you? Just look out the window. The rain. The trees. There's a fringe over everything. A fringe dividing us from the true reality. If only it would lift…'

'Then what?' Gary felt confused and uneasy. 'What would we see?'

'I don't know. But maybe today… with the train. I mean, when the sun breaks through, maybe the fringe will peel away and our eyes will be bathed in light. And everything will be different.' Alan looked at him. His eyes were filled with a dark, incomprehensible longing.

'Maybe. I wish I understood what you're getting at with these things. Maybe we'd be closer if…' Alan wasn't listening. He'd turned back to the window.

Gradually, as the train rumbled past Godalming and Elstead without stopping, the black shelf of cumulonimbus began to dissolve. Strands of rain whipped and broke in the uncertain light. For no apparent reason, a flock of crows rose from a pale cornfield and scattered like fragments of a torn cloud. Fragile threads of golden light reached through the gloom, stroking Gary's eyes. He began to weep.

A moment later, the rain was back and the carriage was full of stale twilight, like a second-hand bookshop. Gary blinked; his eyes stung as if he were looking through smoke.

Alan was sitting with his head in his hands. His face was a charcoal sketch. Gary felt a powerful impulse to touch him; but he didn't move. 'Are you okay?' he said gently.

'Gary, I saw it.' The younger man's eyes were unreadable. 'Not just the sunlight, or the field. I saw the fringe rise over the whole county. It was a vision. I saw… I saw Surrey…'

'…with a fringe on top.'

'…with a fringe on top. Yes.'

There was silence between them. Somewhere, a mobile phone was ringing. Then Alan said quietly, 'I want to die.'

'I know how you feel,' Gary said. 'I really know how you feel. I want you to die too.'

The phone stopped ringing, unanswered. Gary looked past Alan's half-lit face to the window, where a station sign was becoming visible through the rain. It said 'Richmond'. In that moment he knew that the journey, like the silence between them, would never end.

THE LONG SHIFT

There was never enough light. The railway cut through increasingly bare landscapes, bones poking through skin and tearing the white sky like paper, but Jim still felt trapped. The world was an open-plan office. Bilingual signs told him this was another place where he didn't belong. Despite the radiator close to his feet, he was shivering. No room booked. Only one thing gave him a sense of self, and that was carefully hidden between the clothes in his suitcase. He'd used a half-brick to dent and nick the blade so it wouldn't come out clean.

The one thing that had kept him going. That had made him dry out, got him through the puppet-show of rehabilitation, the nights when only vision could keep you alive. Made him come back to the flat and clear out the rubbish, mop the floors, scrub the walls, fight the sense of being poisoned and lost. All the time, one thought: *Baxter.*

No mourners. A cost-effective funeral. Let the gulls scream over Tyseley Dump like fading porn stars. Let the rats creep in the shadows. He had a reason to go on.

Cold sunlight gleamed from mountains too sheer or barren for trees to take hold of them. Darkness had pooled in the valleys where the towns were, creeping up through the woods. From time to time he caught a glimpse of the sea, a wrinkled sheet of tinfoil. Even through the sealed train windows, he could hear the gulls. Everything was directing him towards his purpose. Why else had Baxter moved out here? He had no Welsh past or family that Jim knew of. It was a long journey from the Midlands, for anyone who wanted to find him. Shorter by car, no doubt. But on the train, with every stage along the bare coastline of Cardigan Bay taking you closer to the elements, it was a preparation.

Ritual was everything for Baxter. Timesheets, precise routines, meetings for their own sake. If your socks were the wrong shade of grey he'd call you into his office and say he'd had *comments* from your colleagues. Nothing ever came from him: it was always *a little bird* that had told him. Before each meeting, he briefed his sycophants to make whatever points he wanted to get across. Once he'd ghost-written a whole report damning the performance of another department for a junior editor to read out. No matter how late you'd worked the day before, if you were a few seconds late in the morning he wouldn't speak to you: he'd just tap his watch twice, then turn back to his in-tray.

Coming in midweek gave Jim a better chance of finding Baxter at home, and without visitors. It was a pretty safe bet that Baxter lived alone. His failed marriage was many years in the past, and he referred to his ex-wife as *the error*. To him, all women were *professional victims*. He wasn't keen on men either. He didn't flirt with his staff, let alone chase them. What he liked to do with young employees was impair them: destroy their confidence, their self-respect, their sense of purpose. His weapons of choice were the meeting and the appraisal. That ghostwritten report had gotten Jim's department closed down in a management review of efficiency, but at least he'd never faced a Baxter appraisal. Twelve people had been forced out of the company in nine years by having their efforts trashed in his immaculately typed reports. A few had complained to HR, and HR had advised them to leave.

Night was falling as the train drew into Fishguard. The silhouettes of boats in the harbour were tinged with red. The breeze off the dark water was cold enough to make Jim wish he'd matched his outfit to the bay. Its fresh, salty taste reminded him that he'd eaten nothing since breakfast. He wasn't staying here overnight – that would be too easy to trace – but a quick meal was worth the risk. A few streets away from the station, he found a quiet pub and ordered fish and chips with a glass of Coke. The local beers called to him in melodic accented tones, but he refused to listen. Maybe afterwards, and not here. As he'd expected, the fish was excellent. But maybe his nerves were playing up, because it didn't stay in his system for long. As he sat in a draughty toilet cubicle, pain hollowing his guts, a message stood out from the many inscribed on the back of the door: *There isn't a lorry driver in Fishguard with a drink of fuck to satisfy me.* That cheered him up somewhat.

When he walked back into the twilit bar, the optics added their higher voices to the choir. Jim paused, suitcase in hand,

and let his eyes run across the row of pale, tortured faces behind the barman's head. It was time to go.

———————

Baxter lived in an old famhouse several miles inland of Fishguard. Even if there were a bus, Jim didn't want to be noticed getting off there. His Google map had some worrying blank spots, but the same helpful website's satellite view had shown him the house and barn by daylight: no barbed wire or high railings, only a battered dry-stone wall between the road and the bare farmyard. Somehow, despite the rural setting, Baxter's home had the look of an office: gravel-covered drive, entryphone, Venetian blinds. The barn, only part of which was visible in the photo, appeared to have been sealed up with metal panels. The Welsh Nationalists would have been pretty angry about an English businessman doing that, once upon a time; but maybe their measured doses of self-rule had made them more passive.

Beyond sight of the town, he could still hear the gulls and the dusty vinyl crackling of the sea. The streetlamps became less frequent and then ceased altogether. Jim had to use his small pocket torch to see where he was going. The distant barking of a dog made him break into a sweat. If anything stopped him now, he wasn't sure he'd ever find the nerve to try this again. The weak beam showed him dreamlike glimpses of wire and stonework around fields of Braille. He kept switching it off and then on again every few seconds to save the batteries. But he could never remember what he'd seen, because the afterimage of the torchlight kept resolving itself into the faces from behind the bar. The jury from his dream.

In the dark he cried out: *It wasn't my fault. Don't blame me.*
But there was no response. That was why he'd come here.
Despite the risk, he opened the suitcase a second time and
felt between the shapeless underclothes for the blade. Its
tip cut his finger and he licked the blood, feeling a sense
of renewed control in the taste of his own pain. That was
how nights like this usually went. But this time the haunting
would end. He remembered buying the knife on the way
home from work, after reading Baxter's memo. A small
kitchen knife with a black wooden handle and a razor-sharp
blade. He could see his own eyes reflected in the steel. So far
he'd cut nothing with it except himself.

Gary had been the youngest of Baxter's victims. Everyone
at Neotechnic had liked Gary. He'd been the most helpful
of the IT team, the one who always found the answer but
never made you feel small doing it. A few of the designers
had their eye on him, but he was happily engaged. And then
Baxter took over the design team. Within a month a shadow
had fallen over Gary. He'd seemed nervous, preoccupied,
much less inclined to give people his time. A colleague in
his department said Baxter was 'cracking the whip' on all
of them. And in April, the appraisal season, Gary had been
signed off with stress. Jim knew the union were defending
him in a tribunal, but the details were confidential. Around
that time, Baxter purchased a popular business book called
The Stress Myth and was keeping it on his desk at all times.
Gary lost the tribunal and was dismissed. That kind of thing
was happening a lot and the union seemed unable to do
much about it.

A few weeks later they'd heard that Gary had been found
dead in his flat. Some of his Neotechnic ex-colleagues went

to the cremation, though Baxter made a point of insisting that the usual daily targets had to be achieved. Jim hadn't been able to face going. Funerals left him cold, quite literally: he wondered if the departing spirit took some energy from the mourners to help it cross the black river. He experienced grief as an injury rather than an emotion. No doubt that had to do with him being insane. At the funeral, one of the IT team was told that Gary had left a suicide note in which Baxter's treatment of him was mentioned. The next day, Baxter sent out a memo to the entire site, saying: *Neotechnic will not tolerate irresponsible rumours being spread to the detriment of the Company and its values. Anyone spreading such rumours can expect to be dealt with via the Company's disciplinary procedures.*

After that, Jim had dropped out of the union. He just hadn't seen the point of dragging out more inevitable defeats. When his department was shut down, he'd taken the redundancy cheque with a sense of relief. It had got him out of there after nine years. No more of Baxter sitting vigilant at his desk, like the hawk in the Ted Hughes poem they'd included in an English textbook at school. No more of his mock-weary presence at the end of the day: *You go home. I'm here for the long shift.* It was only later, when Jim had drunk most of the money, that the anger came back. And by then Baxter had taken early retirement, sold his Warwickshire home and relocated to North Wales. He might have been hard to track down if he hadn't put the name of the place on Facebook. *Falcon Lodge.*

As if that memory had a power of its own, the roadway turned upward. In the starlight, Jim could make out bare trees or telegraph poles on either side of the steep hill, and a dark mass ahead. It felt strange to see the stars clear of light pollution, adding to his sense of this being inevitable. The climb made his legs ache. He wanted to hide in the shrubbery, curl up to sleep like a fox. But he'd promised himself the heat of blood on his hands, in his mouth. *Promises to keep.* At last he reached the wall, and checked with his torch: no wire or broken glass along the top, and a few missing stones that would make it easier to get over. The front gate had a tight grid he couldn't hold onto, but that didn't matter. There was no name above the gate, but he could see Baxter's white Volkswagen behind it. Whatever security system the house had wouldn't save Baxter. Jim wasn't there to rob.

His sweat cooled as he paced around the dark wall, and he began to shiver. At the back of the farmyard, the bare ground was muddy and streaked with grass. The barn was alongside the house, a long featureless block part-cased in dull metal. Further out, trees were clustered on a slope that continued upward – he couldn't see what to. The wall would be climbable if he left his suitcase behind, and there wasn't much he needed from it. There were clothes for him to change into later. Stepping carefully over the rough ground, he took the suitcase into the trees and hid it as best he could. Then he crouched for a while, looking up at the house.

Something was moving through the trees behind him, scratching near the ground. It was probably a squirrel, but Jim hastily unfastened his case and took out the knife. He remembered that terrible morning in his Tyseley flat, a few months into his abortive attempt at going freelance. He'd been working late, drinking later. It was a wet autumn day;

he carried his hangover into the kitchen to feed it some painkillers. When he opened the door his first thought was: *What did I do last night?* A bin liner full of rubbish had been torn open and its contents scattered over the floor, including scraps of decaying food. As he'd knelt to pick up the dustpan, something had moved in the nest of black plastic. A grey wedge-shaped head that stared at him for a moment before its owner ran past him into the living room. Where had it gone? He never found out. Traps remained unsprung, trays of poison untouched. He'd kept all the doors shut overnight but still dreamed of rats foraging in the dark, fistfuls of clay that crept over his body and then broke into a foul wet mush.

For weeks he'd barely gone out except to buy alcohol or biscuits, done a few hours of work each evening and spent the rest of the time drinking and watching videos. The work had dried up and he'd run out of films. Friends had tried to help, but he'd ignored them. And then the dream had come. The rat dreams were endless and confused, but *the dream* was crystal clear and happened once only. Like a voice from something inside him that wasn't yet dead. It had made him go to his doctor, spend months on antidepressants, spend the last of his redundancy money on a private alcohol rehab programme. Then he'd come home, sorted out the flat, and started planning the death of Baxter. And now, sitting in the dark among the bare winter trees, he kissed the knife blade and quickly became aroused. Had he needed to want to kill in order to realise it was what he'd always wanted? Whatever, it didn't matter, because what happened to him after killing Baxter didn't matter. He'd stabbed the cunt so many times in his mind, he'd become a serial killer with a single victim.

In the dream, he was falsely convicted of a murder. It had to have been one of two people, and there was no evidence either way, so the court decided on the basis of character witnesses. Those on Jim's side all admitted under questioning that he was a cold bastard who'd let everyone down. He was found guilty and didn't appeal, because the trial had left him feeling his life was worthless. The judge sentenced him to death by lethal injection. The execution took place in a clinic that was part of a railway station, with hundreds of people coming and going. After the injection they set him free, knowing he had less than an hour to live. He wandered around the station and slowly realised the pain, sickness and dizziness were wearing off. The poison had failed. A police officer stopped him, and he told her he wanted to appeal. She said: *It's too late. All you can do is go back to the clinic and let them finish it. The world is a better place without you.* Jim had woken up with the faces of the jury in his mind. They were the twelve people at Neotechnic whom Baxter had forced to leave.

The rustling and scratching in the trees had stopped. Everything was asleep. Jim checked his watch: almost two a.m. No window in the house was lit. He stood up, slipped the knife under his belt and the hammer into his pocket, then wrapped a T-shirt around his left arm and started towards the wall.

There was no sound from within the house, no flicker of light. Jim ran his fingers down the cold glass of a back window. Very carefully, he stretched the T-shirt over the pane and struck it once with the hammer. Fragments of glass stuck to the Venetian blind or trickled onto the carpet. If that had triggered a burglar alarm, the police still wouldn't be here for ten minutes at least. He slashed at the cords of the blind; the plastic slats rattled as they fell. Putting the knife back in his belt, he broke enough glass away to let him climb through. There was no response from inside. The room held a desk, a computer, a few filing cabinets. Had Baxter turned his home into an office?

After the chill of the open road, the central heating was like a blanket wrapped around him. Jim wanted to lie down and sleep. A clock ticked on the wall somewhere. He stepped through into what appeared to be the living room: the pale torch beam showed him a sofa, a monochrome rug, a bookcase. It didn't seem real, didn't seem lived in. But he couldn't expect other people to be as untidy as him. To one side, a staircase ran up the wall. It was uncarpeted, but there was no point in creeping. He didn't want to kill a sleeping Baxter anyway. Painfully aroused, he pushed open the first door on the narrow landing. A web of starlight in frosted glass; a long bath like a sarcophagus. The next room had a wardrobe, a chest of drawers, a single bed by the window. Knife in hand, Jim ran the torch beam up the crumpled duvet to the pillow, which bore the imprint of a head. He cried out with frustration.

Baxter must have got up after hearing the window break. He'd be downstairs, probably armed. So be it. There was no going back. Jim could smell the man's expensive aftershave in the small bedroom. And what the aftershave had hidden: the smell of Baxter. He wasn't aroused any more, just tense with cold rage. This was one meeting where the boss couldn't dictate the outcome. The trapped voice of the water-pipes moaned as Jim paced through the still house. No sign of him. Was he hiding to wait for the police? Increasingly desperate, the intruder ran back and forth, looking for alcoves and doors. Then he noticed a pile of boxes at the back of the staircase that wasn't flush with the wall. Baxter could have squeezed in there. He played the torch along the floorboards. Nothing. An irregularity in the bare wall made him look again. Just an inch from the floor, a tiny wooden knob.

It was a cupboard, but the back had been hollowed out into a narrow passage. The torch light was waning. He crawled into the space, which led downward beneath the floor level. If Baxter had come this way, he must have lost some weight. After a few yards the passage began to curve back upwards. He climbed painfully, unable even to kneel, until he reached a sheer brick surface. Was this a trap? Was the tunnel about to fill with rats? He reached upwards and touched a wooden panel, pressed and felt it give way. Dazed with relief, he stood up and climbed out into what he immediately sensed was another indoor space. He shone the flickering torch around him.

In the middle of the tiny room, a figure sat at a bench. It was a young woman, dressed in faded green overalls, her hair tied back. She was operating some kind of lathe. There were some panels of metal on the bench to the left of the machine, and some thinner strips to the right. The failing torch light glittered from metal shavings scattered over the room. The figure was quite lifelike, except that her eyes were shut. As well, Jim noticed, her left arm was badly twisted and her face had a dull blue tinge. There were smears of

143

dried blood on her frozen hands. Was the model plastic or wax? He reached up and touched its curved neck. It was flesh, cool but not cold. He put his fingers to the motionless lips and felt a trace of breath.

I'm sorry, he whispered. He should call the police – and he would, once he'd done what he came to do. It was a long shift but soon he'd be clocking off, and what happened to him then wouldn't matter. He scanned the walls, which were lined with recent brickwork, and saw a narrow doorway behind the lathe. The door was open. He stepped around the bench, feeling scraps of metal crunch under his feet.

The next room was the same size. It held a desk where a teenage boy was frozen in the act of answering the phone. His immaculate business suit contrasted with his torn and clumsily stitched face. The grey plastic receiver was an inch from his swollen mouth. On the desk, a single bloodstained tooth lay on a pile of memos like a minimal paperweight. On the wall was a square clock, its luminous hands giving the time as half past two.

This must be the barn, Jim realised. No wonder it was sealed from the outside. The third room was almost completely filled with a tangle of black wires and pulleys. A giant toothed wheel was outlined against the wall. turning slowly. The whole system was in gradual motion. Two pale youngsters in shapeless protective clothing were almost buried within the machinery, their limbs contorted and broken. It wasn't clear whether they were driving the machinery or it was driving them.

How many more rooms could there be? Jim bit his lip as he stepped through the doorway, afraid he would scream and alert the museum's curator. But the next room was empty. Through the doorway on the far side, a faint light was gleaming. He paused, allowing himself one more moment of ritual, raised the knife and brushed his lips against its twisted blade. The torch battery was nearly dead: he pressed hard on the switch with his left thumb, trying to hold onto his vision.

This was the only room with plastered walls. There was even a curtain where there could not be any window. On a black leather sofa with red cushions, Baxter was lying asleep. He was dressed but looked almost childlike, at peace with the world. He had indeed lost some weight. Trying not to breathe, Jim stepped forward. He pressed the point of the knife into the soft hollow of Baxter's throat, then tapped on the sleeper's arm to wake him up.

Baxter's eyes opened and he looked up at Jim, then past him, as the intruder felt hands grip his arms from behind and twist hard. A boot came down inside his calf – a *dead leg*, they'd called it in his schooldays – and he fell to his knees, shuddering with pain. Baxter looked down at him and tapped his watch twice, then turned away as the beating started.

INTERNAL COLONIES

Robert had been worked up about it all week. There was a vibration coming off him like a dog that had sniffed a bitch, waiting for his chance. He'd been home a lot, standing in the kitchen or the stairwell like he was practising some Territorial Army manoeuvre. Dad thought he was wound up because he was expecting to hear from them. But Steve knew it had to do with the weekend. When Mum and Dad were going away. The boys were under strict instructions: no parties, no drinking, no pills. But he was sure Robert had something in mind. From the shadow on his face, it might be something he wasn't really looking forward to.

On Friday, Steve had running practice after school. Twice round the city reservoir, where green shrubs and creepers were tangled above the stinking mud. Coming home he felt high; the trees along Yardley Road seemed gigantic in the sticky light of the streetlamps. Each pattern of leaves was like a window into a secret kind of night. When he got home he found that his parents had already taken off. Robert was watching TV with the light off, drinking K cider. He had three bottles lined up on the glass table in front of the couch. Billy was curled in the far corner of the room, a dark comma. His huge eyes tracked Steve's movement from the doorway to the armchair.

Robert fried two steaks for dinner, and sent Steve out for some chips. They ate watching *True Lies* on video. Beside him on the couch, Robert's face was a mask in the half-light. Billy whinged all through the film, nosing at the table until Robert ordered him to keep still. 'I'll feed him later,' he said. 'A bit of hunger's good for a dog. Suppose there's a break-in. You want your dog to rip out the fucker's throat, not roll over and let the thief tickle his belly.' Billy seemed to get the message; for a while afterwards, Steve could hear him pacing up and down the hallway, growling deep in his throat.

It reminded him of the time he'd done a paper round in Fox Hollies. One summer day, there were two Alsatians in the glass-walled passage at the front of a house. As Steve approached the letterbox, they went mad: throwing themselves at the glass, snarling, their legs stiff as railings. One of them tore the *Mail* from his hand and started to destroy it. Lots of the houses round here had signs like REMAINS WILL BE PROSECUTED or DO YOU FEEL LUCKY? Some people had a sign even when they didn't have a guard dog.

Later that evening, two of Robert's friends came round. James who'd been at school with Robert, and Lee from cadets. Lee had a cold in his eyes, and kept dabbing at them with a tissue. They were too broke to go to the pub, so James went out for some cans of Pulse cider. 'We've got things to talk about,' Robert said. 'Grown-up stuff.' Ordinarily Steve would have made a sarcastic comment, but he sensed Robert was in the wrong mood for that. Passing the dull shadow of Billy on the stairs, he went up to his room and played the new Pulp album on his portable CD player. It was strange, like being lost. Pointless and a bit frightening. The woman on the CD cover was nice, though. He turned the light off and imagined she was in the room, bent over, her arse towards him.

When the album finished, he sat there in the dark, looking out of the window. The back garden was full of rubbish and twisted black trees. Downstairs, they were watching *Commando* on video. It was Robert's favourite film. During one of the quiet bits, he heard the three of them laughing and Lee saying: *Seriously? That fucking kid?* More laughter, then Robert said: *Why the fuck not? He'll never tell.*

Eventually, he heard them leave. Robert came up to the bathroom and pissed for about nine minutes, then went to bed. Steve drifted into an uneasy sleep. Later, he heard a girl's voice. He thought it came from his dream, but then he heard Robert's voice. They were downstairs. The blue display on his alarm clock read 03:12. Where the fuck had Robert found someone at this time of night? As they stumbled into Robert's bedroom, Steve bit his finger and listened intently for the sounds. But all he heard was shoes dropping, then silence. And then a female cry that seemed to mix rage and fear. Then feet on the stairs, Robert coming down after her, her shouting *Fuck off*.

149

The front door slammed. Then Robert went back into his room. Through the dark, Steve heard him wanking. It sounded more like he was in pain.

———————

The next evening, Robert stayed in and watched cable TV with Lee and Steve. Lee still had infected eyes. On the screen, dark-skinned topless women floated like shadows through a nightclub; thugs spat blood against brick walls. Billy stared imploringly at Robert, then at Steve. 'He's a good dog,' Steve said. 'What's the point of starving him?' Robert shook his head. Billy went out into the hallway and paced up and down manically, whining. Lee and Robert had some cans of White Lightning, but they didn't seem in any hurry to drink them.

Around midnight, Robert said: 'Steve, in a bit, we're going out to do some dog training. James is bringing Hawk... and something else. You got two choices. Either you go to bed and forget you heard anything, or you come with us and forget you saw anything. What's it going to be?' The light from the screen flickered on his still face.

'I'll come with you,' Steve said. He felt a tension pulling inside him that he supposed was like what Robert felt. He was sharing their secret. They drank some coffee and watched a Spanish porn movie without subtitles. There were whips. Steve was glad the darkness hid his reaction. Then they drank some more coffee. It made him feel like bits of ash were floating in his bloodstream.

It was nearly three o'clock when Robert stood up. 'Come on, men. All stations ready for action.' He fitted the lead on

Billy's tense neck. Outside, the streets were empty. Steve could hear cars going by on the Warwick Road. It had been raining earlier; the streetlamps painted the trees with wet light. Lee and Robert were wearing camo jackets. Steve thought it made them stand out, but he kept his mouth shut. Security lights flashed on them as they passed some of the houses. He watched his own shadow doubled, cast sideways and in front of him.

Near the top of Pool Farm Road, the park fell away into the night. A chain of lights stretched out like ships on a black sea. They walked down along the footpath, then turned left through the trees. The ground smelt of rain and new growth. Moonlight shone vaguely through shattered windows of leaves. Steve remembered bright days from his childhood here: spinning on the roundabout, playing soccer with a plastic ball, watching dogs run for sticks. Billy was restless, pawing at the ground. Suddenly he changed direction and pulled Robert down the slope towards the railings that surrounded the tiny lake. Robert held on tight, but let himself be guided. The others stumbled after them.

A few yards ahead, a dog barked. A pale torch came on. Its beam lit Billy's face, then Robert's. 'You're late.' It was James. The dog with him was Hawk, the black terrier.

'You got it? The bait?' Lee said. James picked up a bin liner with something in it. They walked on to the far side of the lake, where even the torch would be hidden from the road. This was the area of the park where Steve always liked to imagine he was in a wilderness, miles from anywhere. He could see moonlight glinting on the lake, a tree caught in a nest of creepers. The cold wind stiffened his hair.

'Took me fucking ages. Better be worth it.' James handed the bin liner to Lee, who spread it on the ground while the other two held onto their dogs. The black plastic rippled and slid back, releasing a heap of reddish jelly. Knots of dried blood and tufts of fur clung to its surface. From what remained of its face, Steve could see it was a cat. He bit his tongue; the stink of nearly fresh meat made him start to retch. The dogs snarled as they were dragged back into the trees.

Lee knelt and pointed his torch towards the bait. Steve swallowed the thread of bile that had crept into his mouth. They waited. He could feel water creeping from the ground into his flimsy shoes. The dogs were tense, but quiet. Maybe they felt at home here. More time passed. Lee kept sniffing and wiping his nose on his hand. The moon slipped from cloud to cloud, backing off. Robert glanced at his watch and whispered: 'Two hours at most. I wish we had guns.' James unscrewed a metal hip-flask, swigged from it and passed it round. Steve took a cautious sip; it exploded in his mouth like a smoky flame.

Eventually the moon disappeared behind the trees at the roadside. The stars were clouded over, but a vague bell of reflected light hung over the city. Steve was shifting from foot to foot, trying to fight off cramp. Then Lee whispered, *Fuck*. In the half-light of the dying batteries, a dark shape was moving. He switched off the torch. Steve heard a grunt, then the slobbering noises of an animal feeding. Together, Robert and Lee whispered: *Three, two, one – go!* They released the dogs. Steve heard a volley of barking and a thin, terrible scream. Then Lee switched the torch back on.

The two dogs were crouched over the fox, shaking and tearing it. Their feet scrabbled in the ruins of the wet bait.

Hawk had ripped open the fox's belly and was eating what fell out. One of its back legs was splayed at an angle, brown fur hanging from an edge of bone. Billy's teeth were fixed in its throat, shuddering until the fox's blood gushed over his muzzle and collar. The fox released a stream of yellow shit like a second tail, then died. The dogs went on tearing at the mixture of fox and cat: faceless, nameless, burnt. The boys watched until the torch finally lost its strength.

When they went to pull the dogs away from what remained, Steve hung back. He watched Robert pick up Billy's lead and wipe the blood and shit off it. If he kept his mouth shut, he wouldn't puke. The figures, human and animal, were no more than blobs of darkness against the grey of the first morning light. Robert came back towards him, pointing to the rubble of blood and bones. 'That's a burglar,' he said. 'That's a fucking tea-leaf. Mission accomplished.' Then he walked on towards the lake. Billy trotted after him, stinking.

They got both dogs to wash in the scummy lake. That impressed Steve more than anything else. Then James and Hawk took off for home, using the Gospel Lane exit from the park. The rest of them went up to the Shirley Road end, walking calmly along like a family on an early morning stroll. The children's playground was a sketch: tyre, climbing-frame, roundabout. There were a few cars on the roads, but no one else was walking.

Back at the house, Billy slumped in the corner. He looked shattered. 'Well done, soldier,' Robert murmured. He and Lee cracked open cans of cider. Steve declined the offer of a fresh can. He sat back in the armchair, watching the other two drink and relax. He felt at home. As the dawn light framed the edges of the curtains, he fell asleep. Some time later, Robert guided him up the stairs to bed.

When Steve emerged from the tangled undergrowth of sleep, it was getting dark outside. Robert and Lee were downstairs, watching *The Rock* or something like it. The room smelt of sweat, cider and dog. 'Whatever I do,' Robert was saying, 'I want to get away from here.'

'Me too,' Lee said. 'It's no good here. Too many fucking Micks for my liking. There's probably enough Semtex stashed away in basements in Acocks Green to blow up the whole city. Thought I might go to Germany. Or Northfield, if I get that job at Longbridge.' He sniffed. 'You heard from the TA yet?'

'No.' It had been a long time. 'That'd be crap anyway. The Army's fucked. We used to be out there, ruling the colonies. Now the fucking colonies are here.'

'True. And they won't even let you keep a gun.' Lee sighed. 'This is worse than a hangover. Still, it was worth it, right?'

'What was?' Robert looked blank. 'Steve, do you know what he's talking about?'

'No idea.' Steve huddled in the armchair, enjoying the warmth of the living room. Explosions flared on the screen. Blood painted a villain's mouth like lipstick.

When the film ended, Robert and Lee went out. 'Tell Mum and Dad I'll be back later. Don't know how late.' That gave Steve a chance to do what he'd been waiting to do for weeks. He'd got the idea from his friend Dennis in school. *I bet he's got magazines. Look under the clothes in his chest of drawers. Or at the back of his wardrobe.* Robert's bedroom was nearly bare, like a hotel room where someone had just spent the night. Steve left the door open so he'd hear if anyone came.

First he tried the chest of drawers. Nothing of interest, except a sealed packet of condoms. Then the wardrobe: a stack of war and true crime magazines. Further back, two carrier bags with more magazines; as he turned the upper bag, a few slipped out. *Nightshade*, *Black Bottom*, *Service*. They all had topless black women on the cover. He picked one up, saw the pages were rippled. He let it fall open. The stain was just beyond the centrefold. A blackish crust over the glossy brown flesh of a woman's neck and shoulders. Some dry flakes broke from the page.

In the next magazine, the stain obliterated a whole face. In the next, bloodstains were scattered all the way through, marking breasts and crotches like a tacky underwear design. He supposed Robert was using his own blood. Whatever. He didn't want to know. Carefully, he squeezed the magazines back into the carrier bag and put it on top of the other one, behind the dusty stack of war magazines. Then he closed the wardrobe door and quit his brother's room.

At once, he felt anxious. Surely Robert would know his things had been messed with. That room was so tidy, a moth couldn't cross it without leaving traces. He'd better make sure he was out when Robert got back. Once Mum and Dad were home, Robert would have to wait; then he'd calm down. Putting on his ski jacket, Steve left the house. Billy was still asleep in his box by the stairs.

Outside, it was raining lightly. Gusts of wind scratched the roofs of cars. He walked past the Great Western pub, where a woman was leaving and a man was trying to pull her back. Their voices blew away. Out beyond the railway bridge, it was quiet. He shivered. Cars drove towards him, their windscreens scarred with rain. A memory from last night came back to him: the fox's head with a few inches of spine attached to it, like an electric carving knife. Had he really seen that? The long sleep in between made it seem unreal.

He walked on. A dog howled from near the canal, and another called back. Territory. What did that mean? Or else mating. Suddenly a much older memory came to him: the playground at junior school. Two dogs had wandered in off the street and were fucking in the sunlight. He remembered how still they'd been, every muscle taut. Like one of those terrible cramps that woke you up and made you feel skinless.

It was colder than last night, as cold as winter. As he walked on past the white statues of the Yardley cemetery, he thought he could still hear the two dogs calling to each other across the canal. The echo would never become real, or fade.

AMONG THE LEAVES

The caravans had moved on. The nearly circular car park to the right of the disused pub was empty, except for a few heaps of brick and litter. Behind the car park, a fringe of trees was on fire with age; it seemed to be giving off the factory smoke Kay could see in the distance, slowly uncoiling against a pale sky. She wondered if the gypsies had gone of their own accord, or been forced out. Kay hadn't been here in— what, six months? For all she knew, Janet had moved on. But if she was still with Mark, perhaps they'd settled down.

Janet's flat was in the house around the corner from the pub – which had previously been boarded up, but whose doors and windows were now bricked over. The house had no front garden or gate. Kay rang the lower of the two unmarked bells. The door opened to the length of a security chain.

'Who's there?'

'Janet? It's me, Kay.'

The chain rattled free. Janet looked tired but otherwise unchanged. She'd always been pale, her eyes charged with unease even when she laughed. They'd worked together in a chemist's shop for several months, until Kay had got a job as a receptionist with the Accident Hospital.

'Come in,' Janet said. In the living room, boxes and large packages wrapped in brown paper were stacked against the walls. 'I'm leaving in a week's time,' she explained. 'Going to Bradford. I don't like to stay in one place too long.' She looked at Kay. 'Now Ian's dead, I think I need to move on. Make a clean break. You know.'

Kay nodded, confused. 'I'm sorry.' She wanted to ask who Ian was. Had Janet mentioned him before? In the silence, she could hear a tape playing quietly on the far side of the room, where the glass door framed an overgrown garden. She recognised R.E.M.'s *Document*. Janet offered to make some coffee, and Kay said, 'Please.' Apart from some furniture and the cassette player, everything in the living room was packed. Kay sat at one end of the couch and waited.

When Janet came back, they talked about the chemist's shop and Kay's new job. Then Janet said, 'I don't know what I'll do in Bradford. Got enough saved up to get by for a month or so. I'll improvise. It usually works out. I've been moving every two or three years since I left home.' She looked about thirty years old, allowing for the youthfulness that rootless people always seemed to have. 'Ian and I lived together for nine years,' she said quietly. 'You never met him, did you? We tended to keep our social lives separate. Too much, really. We shouldn't have been so afraid. If only we hadn't looked so similar… Everything else, we could get round.'

There was a pause. Kay said, 'What happened to him?'

'Crossing the road, drunk, late at night. He got hit by a car. I had to identify him.' Her face seemed to shut in on itself, like a newspaper folding. 'We were twins. Maybe, with time, it would have been all right. Not to hide it, I mean. It wasn't as if we had children. Or were going to. But when you start off feeling guilty about something, the effects can last the whole of your life.'

'I'm sorry you felt like that. It was your life after all.' But sometimes, Kay knew, people could only see a word. And there was still something she didn't understand. 'What happened with you and Mark?'

Janet stared at her as if trying to remember something. The movement of clouds in the window made her face appear to shiver. 'Mark who?' she asked. 'I don't know anyone called Mark... at least not well. You must be thinking of Alison or someone else at the shop.' Kay was familiar with the porcelain blankness that people showed when lying. Janet's expression was different. She looked genuinely confused; and there was something there that Kay didn't recognise. It was like seeing a figure in silhouette behind a stage curtain, not knowing its actual size or its distance from the screen. Janet got up and switched the tape over; it had finished while they were talking.

'Yes, I'm sorry,' Kay said. 'It must be Alison. I've lost touch a bit...' The room was cold; she rubbed her hands together, then stood up. Behind Janet's head, she could see a tree rusting down to its skeleton. She thanked Janet for the coffee, wished her good luck in Bradford, and then – as an afterthought – asked her if she could use some help with the move.

Janet hesitated, perhaps unsure whether it was a real offer or just a polite noise. Then she smiled. 'Thank you, yes. That would be great. It shouldn't take long. I've hired a van – if you could help me load it, I'll give you a lift home, then carry on to Yorkshire.'

They arranged a time, then said goodbye. Outside, the light was thinning; the rain shadowed the pavements and touched the dead leaves with colour. On the main road, the traffic heading into town seemed to be at motorway speed. When the lights at the corner changed, two cars jolted to a halt – one just inside the line, the other halfway over it. It would be better to go miles out of your way, Kay thought, than to turn right onto this stretch of road. Which route would the van take? She was still thinking about it, and about some other things, when the bus came.

———————

The empty playground just inside the park gates was like a negative for the park's colour print. Janet walked around the edge, inside the darkening barrier of trees. Wasn't it next weekend the clocks were going back? Leaves rustled under her feet like newspaper; there was a smell of smoke, but it was only three boys in grey school uniform, sharing a cigarette. They were sitting on a bench, passing the light between them like a blazing eye. Through the trees ahead, she could see the Morse code of passing traffic. A flock of starlings clustered above the highest tree, shivering in unison.

The silence pulsed in her head. Back in the flat, she'd been playing old records for hours, afraid to be alone with her thoughts. Kay's visit had helped, though talking about Ian was less a release than a coming back to reality. She was glad to be leaving the flat; it was draughty in winter and the walls were thin. The house was gradually subsiding, which was why the landlord couldn't sell it. She'd read in a local paper that the whole of north Birmingham was sinking, reverting to the pre-industrial marshland. Homes never lasted long.

There were more trees at the end of the park than she'd thought; dead leaves covered the pathway, soft masses under dry skins. The reddish light of sunset reflected in some broken glass near her feet. Janet remembered an incident from her childhood: Ian hiding in a pile of dead leaves and waiting for her, then jumping out. For a moment she could imagine brushing a leaf from his hair. Darkness grabbed at her from between the trees. What had happened to the road?

As she stood confused, beginning to tremble, some leaves fell against her coat. One lodged against her neck, dry as paper; she lifted it and held it up to the light. Its veins showed red through the brittle tissue. Some blood dripped from the base of the leaf onto Janet's hand. She closed her eyes as the darkness gripped her arms and shook her.

Mark lived in Shard End, a long bus ride out through council estates that were like a child's construction kit, most of the pieces having been trodden on or lost. Flat shopping arcades, encased in shells of concrete, were coiled around pale and glassy-eyed tower blocks. Small fragments of routine life were visible amongst the marks of violence and neglect: a window box, clothes on a washing line, the cocked ear of a satellite dish. In many buildings, the only occupants were squatters.

Shard End itself was slightly more reassuring: terraced houses painted in various colours; trees whose heads were turning to gold; a primary school so heavily armoured it might have been a military barracks. Kay wasn't sure if Mark still lived there. It was only by coincidence that she had the address: Mark and Susan, Kay's girlfriend, had both done a film studies course at the technical college a year ago. Mark had held a party at his flat; Kay and Susan had both gone. So had Janet, Kay remembered suddenly.

The door to Mark's flat was inside the passage between two houses. Kay paused before ringing. Perhaps coming here was a mistake. Surely it was none of her business. And if Mark was living with somebody else, he might not want to talk about Janet. Only the thought that if she gave up now she would have wasted a journey made her press the doorbell. Mark answered almost at once. 'Um… hello?' Of course, he probably didn't recognise her.

'Hi, it's Kay. I live with Susan. We came to your party…' Kay had the feeling of trying to impose connections on too many disparate elements, like a bad fortune-teller.

'Oh God, yes,' Mark said. 'Come in. How are you doing?' His flat looked scruffy but creative: posters and album covers on the walls, magazines heaped in one corner, several brands of whisky on a shelf above the gas fire. Mark offered her a choice of coffee or beer. She took a can gratefully, and poured from it while thinking about what to say. 'Louise should be back soon,' Mark said. 'My girlfriend. She moved in three months ago.'

'Is she colour blind?' Kay asked.

'What?… Oh, you mean the curtains. They were in a sale. We call them the wedding present. Because they're too loud and out of tune.' Kay laughed and began to relax. They talked about Susan: her job doing posters for the local arts centre, and the novel she was halfway through writing. Mark was training to be a car repairer. What use was a film studies course in a country where people thought all films came from Hollywood?

There wasn't much time, Kay realised. And she hadn't explained why she was here. 'I hate to dredge up your past,' she said, 'but I wanted to ask you about something. You remember Janet?' He nodded, his eyes fixed on her. 'I saw her yesterday. She's leaving the area. I mentioned you and… I swear she doesn't remember you. She didn't recognise your name.' Mark didn't react. 'I think there's something the matter with her, and I just… wanted to know, do you know anything that might help? Is there anything I could do?'

Mark thought for a couple of minutes. 'I can't explain it,' he said finally. 'When we split up, it was amicable enough. I thought her reasons were a bit odd. She said she was used to living alone. Didn't want to change that. And she said she was going to move on from Birmingham soon. From some people, I would have regarded all that as bull. You know, just a way of saying *I don't want you*. But she really seemed to mean it. And then there was something about her brother.'

'Her brother?' The room seemed to draw inward. 'You mean Ian?'

'That's right, yes. He died when they were fourteen. I've seen a photo of him. She told me… well, his death seems to have affected her quite badly. Changed her emotions somehow, I don't know. You would have thought after this long…'

Kay suddenly wished she was somewhere else. Anywhere else. 'She told me he died… quite recently. I don't get it. Is she reliving his death?' Mark didn't answer. 'Maybe if… do you think, if we both went to see her…?'

Mark shook his head. 'It might make things worse. And I don't have the right. I don't want to sound like I'm avoiding it because I used to go out with her, but I realised when we split up that I just *didn't belong* in her life, it was like a different country.' He stood up and looked out of the window, gripping his arms tensely. Poplar trees flickered above the black rooftops, glowing faintly with reflected light. Tiny silhouettes of birds rose and fell in the distance.

Then he turned back. 'If Janet's coping at the moment,' he said, 'it might be wrong to interfere. Sometimes when you take away the belief, the darkness crashes through. It's like that Bergman film Susan and I watched at college. There's a girl in that who thinks she's having visions of God. When she realises it isn't God, she's just hallucinating, everything is destroyed for her. If Janet obviously needed help, it would be different. But even then, we wouldn't know what to do.' Kay tried to read his expression but the window was behind him, casting his features into shadowed relief. The room was growing dark.

On the way home, the bus stopped for a while outside Lightwoods Park. Kay watched children playing football among trees that jittered like a loose slide in a projector. It occurred to her that Janet might not just be imagining the things she said. Perhaps her brother was making her think them. Kay looked away from the trees; they seemed magnified in the half-light. As the bus jolted back to life and started down the long hill towards Harborne, she wondered if it made any difference.

———————

There was one thing left, and it wouldn't take long. The roads were busy, but there was hardly anyone out on the pavement. Janet rubbed the sleeves of her coat together. Beyond the grey car park, colours were beginning to soak through the trees. She stepped over the remnant of a brick wall and across a rockery of litter to some wasteground that must once have been somebody's garden. The trees she'd seen from the road were mostly here. On the far side, the canal was stepped a long distance uphill into Aston. The three largest trees made a nearly regular triangle, at the centre of which was a mound of dead leaves about three feet high. It had taken her weeks to collect them all.

Now it was time. She took the can of butane fuel from her coat pocket and unscrewed the lid, then poured the colourless fluid onto the mound. It spread like frost, its vapour stiffening the air. Some leaves had blown away and were scattered around the edge of the pile. Janet leaned down and picked up a few of them. Their frozen edges cut her hand. She wiped the blood on the dark sleeve of her coat, and struck a match. Her mind was blank.

The flames crept over the mound, blue tinged with pale yellow. Janet felt her recent memories darken and blur; within her, something older turned over to face the light. Mum opening the bedroom door and staring. Janet trying to hide under the blanket. Ian just lying there, face upward, unable to move. Then Mum stepping forward and hitting

Ian repeatedly across the face, screaming at them both. Ian getting dressed, his hands shaking as he wiped blood from his mouth and nostrils. Janet hiding in her room, in the dark, playing the same tape over and over again.

The mound of leaves was shrinking, clotting together. Her mouth filled with the smell of things burned by fuel, things that weren't dry enough to burn alone. The smoke hung like a blotched net curtain across the trees and the distant buildings.

They found him on the railway embankment, among the leaves. He'd cut his left wrist with a razor blade, then tried to cut his right one but been unable to, because the tendons of his left hand were damaged. The police said it had to be suicide. Nobody touched him, they said.

The leaves were blackened, their edges white with ash. The fire was gone; but outside the shadow of the trees, sunlight warmed the still air. In the street, people were opening their shops, raising canopies and putting out displays. That was all. That was it, for the time being. She turned back to the house, where Kay was waiting to help her load the van.

THE GRIEF OF SEAGULLS

The fish will fly and the seas go dry
The rocks will melter in the sun
The working men will forget their labour
Before I do return again
– Traditional

The quay was nearly deserted. Only a few old men standing outside the pubs, gazing out to sea as the evening light faded. One of them looked familiar. Maybe I'd seen him at the Duthie Park memorial, though I didn't go there much. Here was where I went to be with Andrew. When I looked across the metallic water, the image was still there: so clear I could believe it was imprinted on the landscape, not just on my memory. The crimson fireball of a burning oil rig.

I walked from the station to the harbour, which was choked with steel Halliburton ships and grey oil tanks. At least the company had changed. Further on, the oil vessels thinned out until I could see across the harbour to a finger of bare land where temporary buildings stood behind wire fences. The pebble beaches were mostly pink granite, as if they had soaked up blood from the water. Out at sea, I could just make out a line of black rocks like burial mounds. Seagulls flew out and back again in long swooping arcs, greeting like weans.

Andrew had been working on the Piper Alpha rig for three months. He'd told me the American oil company was trying to make workers leave the union. They'd stopped safety training because it reduced productivity. We don't believe in red tape, the site manager had said. He didn't like it, but jobs were hard to come by. We were saving for a flat. It still wasn't long since they'd changed the law – we had to be furtive, but at least we weren't facing jail for sharing a bed.

That day, I was working in the shop when the news came through that Piper Alpha was on fire. I had to wait until my lunch break to run down to the quay and see the rig in the distance, wreathed in flames. A carpet of burning oil surrounded it. Helicopters were circling above the fire, looking for a place to land. I walked back to the shop. Half an hour later, I heard a dull boom, felt the walls shake. I walked slowly to the staff toilet and threw up, then went back to the till.

That evening I was one of hundreds of people waiting at the infirmary. Some were praying or greeting newcomers, but most were silent. Of a hundred and sixty men only a few dozen had come back alive, and it was rumoured they were terribly burned from the oil: crippled, faceless, blinded. Andrew's parents were there too, and his sister. She knew about us but they didn't, so I had to keep quiet. But I didn't have to hide my tears in the middle of so much grief. Ambulances were coming back with only dead men inside, or none at all. I went home at three in the morning. It was hard to walk. I'd not have believed emptiness could weigh so much.

It came out in the inquiry that after the fire had started, the site manager in Aberdeen had twice decided to keep the oil pipe running because the risk of an explosion didn't justify losing a day's income. The company escaped prosecution because too little evidence had survived the wreckage.

Tears were blurring my view as I turned back towards the quay. There wasn't much to look at anyway: distant streetlights in the town, a few vessels out at sea. Once Andrew and I had walked out here, hand in hand, and seen a twisted blue-green shape hanging in the night sky. But tonight there were no visions. Only a small dark figure on the quayside, making its way towards me.

It was the old man from the pub by the station. Had he followed me all the way out here? I wondered if he'd seen me in Oh Henry's some time. If so, I wasn't in the mood. There'd been other men since Andrew – it had been twelve years, after all – but tonight belonged to him. The seagulls cried louder as I stood and waited. So near the sea's dark mass, the night was chilly. I could smell oil on the pebbles.

He stopped a few feet away from me. I couldn't see his face clearly, though I remembered it: white hair around a clean-shaven, rather gaunt face, a man of sixty or so. 'I'm sorry to intrude,' he said.

'It's a public right of way,' I answered. 'You're not intruding unless you bother me. I'd recommend not.'

'I lost someone too,' he said. 'In the disaster, the fire. I wondered if maybe we could talk.'

'I'm not big on support groups.' But as I spoke, I could feel the story's weight inside me. Could it be shared? 'Look, if I tell you – whatever you hear, it stays with you. Understood?'

'Of course.' He touched my arm gently. Close up I could hear a faint wheeze on his breath. Maybe he was ill. We walked back to the quay and I told him about Andrew. How we met, how we became lovers, our plans. And then that long day. The burning rig on the horizon. The night at the infirmary, waiting. The funeral with an empty coffin.

By the time I'd finished, we'd walked past the station and onward towards Balmedie. The old man was silent; so were the gulls. 'What's your story?' I asked.

'It's late,' he said. 'I'm older than you'd think. Need to rest. Meet me here tomorrow and I'll tell you what happened. Nine o'clock on the quay, outside the Moorings. Can you make it?' I nodded. He looked fit to drop, and I was worn out from the long walk. His thin hand gripped my shoulder. 'See you.'

It wasn't closing time yet, but I was too tired for a pub. The sea twitched and shook restlessly, a blanket over a sleeping body. I walked home, poured myself some whisky and fell asleep with the glass still in my hand.

The next evening was brighter: the sky held a faint glow, like granite. I was in no mood for company, but the old man had listened to me. There were a few men standing outside the

Moorings on Trinity Quay, smoking, but he wasn't among them. I went into the pub, bought a dram of Laphroaig and drank it straight off. It tasted of ashes – but then, it always does. There were pictures of old sailing ships on the walls. When I walked back outside, another man had arrived. Not the one I was waiting for, though he looked vaguely familiar. There were faint scars over his face and neck.

Then he looked at me. 'Callum?' I nodded, wondering if the old man had sent him. But we hadn't exchanged names. And this stranger could be my age, though the scars made it hard to tell. It was like a fine pale cobweb over his skin. He held out his hand, which was similarly marked. 'Good to see you,' he said. Not wanting to be rude, I shook his hand. His thin fingers tightened their grip, and suddenly I knew.

'Did he send you?' I asked. He nodded. 'What the fuck?'

'We don't have much time.' His eyes were dark with pain. 'Let's go to the harbour. I've got things to tell you.' The same voice, but quieter – and flawed, as if the scars were internal too. I was shaking as we walked together along the quay. A dull red flame was spreading on the water, but it was only light.

There was nobody at the harbour, where tall grey oil tanks almost blocked out the view. He took my hand again and just held it. I could feel the warmth of his skin. And the scars, a faint Braille I had no idea how to read. 'The oil companies won,' he said. 'They always get what they want.'

I turned to look at him. Then our faces were together and the taste of his kiss was in my mouth, the same as before. His hands on me, our bodies pressing together. He kissed my neck and bit gently, not breaking the skin. I reached up to his chest, slipped my hand between the buttons of his shirt. More scars.

Seagulls were greeting above the oil vessels. I stepped back, staring. 'How did you survive?'

He just shook his head. 'Where have you been?' I asked.

'Under the water. In the stone. Nowhere.' He raised his damaged hands towards me and I stepped forward, let him touch my face. 'And you, Callum? Did you stay here?'

'I moved away. But I had to come back. This is where I belong.' My eyes were blurring. 'God, I've missed you. You don't know…'

'I do,' he said, his mouth almost touching my ear. 'Missing someone can be a place. The city of without.' His hand rested on my belly, moved down. 'Callum, we don't have much time. Is there somewhere we can go? I mean near.'

'Shall we have a look?' I said. We'd done that before, a few times, but not here. We walked out beyond the harbour, to where the quay turned back towards the city. I could see the line of rocks in the water. Most of the buildings were locked up, and some looked derelict. A passageway between two houses was unlit, but didn't smell bad. I touched his arm and stepped backwards into the darkness.

He followed me and pressed me against the wall. I could hear his breathing, louder as I unbuttoned his shirt. His thin hands pulled at my shoulders, gently taking control. I knelt and unzipped his jeans, went down on him. My lips found no scars. His fingers gripped my hair. 'Callum,' he said quietly. I felt him tense, shudder and spurt in my mouth. Twelve years, but his taste was the same.

I stood up and reached for him, but something was changing. The scars on his chest were denser, and they gave way under my hands. I reached up towards his face and could feel only a web of scars, as if that was all that held him together. Glad that I couldn't see anything here, I gripped his torn arms and we pressed together against the wall. I felt a cool breath against my lips. And then my hands and my face were crushed against cold, damp brick.

When I walked back along the quay, night had fallen. A frail aurora was glowing above the black water: a ragged veil of blue and yellow like bruised skin. As I watched, the colours melted into each other and the night. Near the station, I saw the old man sitting asleep on a bench. He looked worn out, as if after a hard day's work. Then I realised what his work was.

I saw him again – the old man, that is – a few weeks later. By then it was autumn, and a bitter wind was blowing in from the iron sea. He and a younger man were walking towards the harbour. As they passed me, deep in conversation, I avoided catching the old man's eye. I didn't want to interrupt his work. Or make him think I was jealous. Or, to be honest, know him.

BY NIGHT HE COULD NOT SEE

The first Jason knew about it was a story in the *Express & Star*. A forty-six-year-old woman had been found dead on a train between Walsall and Aldridge. Cause of death unknown. The only sign of violence was the paint on her face and hands, which might have been daubed on before or after her death. The police wondered if it was linked to cult activity. They gave her name: Gail Warner. There was no photo. At the end of the brief report, the journalist noted that in the last year, two other dead people in the UK had been found smeared with paint in the same way.

It wasn't such an unusual name. He wasn't even sure the age was right, though it was close. If it was the same person, did Mark know about it? They probably hadn't stayed in touch – teenage lovers never did. Jason might have stood a chance with Gail if she hadn't been wrapped around Mark like a pale ribbon. A few times they'd turned up late for a meeting of the Yardbirds, looking flushed and gratified. Jason had bitten through his lip thinking about it, still had the scar. But then Clare had come along and it had ceased to matter.

The gang's name came from Yardley, where they'd all lived. It seemed very distant now, like a film he'd seen in his teens. The Swan Centre, their main stomping-ground, had recently been knocked down. The knot of reeking subways in front of it had been replaced by a concrete walkway over the Coventry Road that trembled from all the cars passing through. Yardley felt more like an airport than a district now. You couldn't stand still without getting vertigo.

Jason felt restless. Being reminded of the past wasn't good for him. But it was too cold to go out for a walk, and he had work tomorrow so the pub wasn't a good idea. He walked around the house, mentally listing the repair tasks that needed his attention, knowing they wouldn't happen any time soon. What you can't sort out, you have to walk away from. But why had he stayed here? The posters he'd put up to cover the damp in the hallway were looking bruised.

The gang hadn't been that bad. Clapton's Yardbirds were probably guilty of worse crimes. At least on record. Most of it was running: handling stuff for the big boys, passing on messages, occasionally breathing down some unwashed neck or helping some no-mark to have a small accident. Nothing to give Richard Allen sleepless nights. Like the Krays, they'd only hurt their own. The hurting had got out of hand. It always did.

Four cigarettes later, he phoned his old mate Darren in Walsall. They'd worked together in a security firm back in the nineties, driving cash and prisoners across the region.

Then Darren had joined the police force. He knew about the Yardbirds – at least, he'd heard the radio edit – but he wasn't the type to moralise. It was all just work to him.

Darren took the call on his mobile. They swapped greetings. As usual, Jason had no recent news. Darren had got divorced, and something bad had happened in Aldridge that he couldn't talk about. Then Jason asked him if he'd heard about the dead woman on the train. 'I think I used to know her. Was she blonde?'

'Not when our pathologist saw her. Someone had smeared green paint on her hair and forehead. There was more paint on her hands, but it was different – a kind of blue, like she was cold. Pastel colours. Skin paint, like they use on stage, not industrial paint. What kind of nutter puts make-up on a dead wench?'

'The paper said it might be a weird cult of some kind. Apparently there were two more deaths like that last year.'

'Not around here, there weren't. But it could be a cult. Some Internet thing maybe. Too few and far between to be connected any other way.'

'This dead woman. What did she look like?'

'Skinny and pale. Her hair was grey. Might have been blonde once.'

'Thanks. It's not the girl I knew.' He wondered if Darren could tell he was lying. 'I'll see you around, mate. Take care.'

'Stay out of trouble, you.' Jason snapped his hinged phone together. The living room door was closed, but the house felt colder than before. The faint ringing in his head might be a distant siren, an echo of static on the phone, or just a headache coming on.

After several failed attempts, his virus-ridden computer

let him access the Web. He searched for the combination of 'dead', 'head and hands' and 'paint'. Most of the links were to academic websites on religious art, but one led him to a story in the *South Wales Evening Post*. A body washed up in Swansea Bay last autumn had been identified as that of Mark Page, a businessman in his forties who'd lived in the city for nine years after leaving Birmingham. Police were unable to explain the traces of paint on his head and hands. They suggested it had to do with cult activity or gang warfare. Either way, drugs were behind it.

Jason switched off his computer and sat in the dark for a few minutes. The phone rang, jarring his skull. He stumbled downstairs and picked up the receiver without speaking. It was Darren. 'Just spoke to a colleague, Theresa, who knows about one of the other cases. The body of a middle-aged man was found on an industrial estate in Manchester, half eaten by rats, with green paint in his hair and blue paint on what was left of his hands. About nine months ago. They never did identify him. Don't suppose you've got any idea who it was?'

'How would I know?' *Tony Matthews.*

'Course not. Silly of me.' Jason flipped his middle finger violently at the damp-stained wall. 'Well, see you around.'

His head was aching so badly he thought he was going to throw up. A few minutes kneeling over the toilet bowl, the chemical odour of the blue disinfectant scouring his nostrils, produced no offering but a trickle of colourless fluid from his mouth. *Mark, Gail, Tony and me.* But something was missing. He'd locked away the memories and they'd rotted in the dark. He needed a key.

No, he needed a drink. There was nothing in the house.

Jason locked his front door with trembling fingers, stared up and down the narrow road. He didn't know what for – but if it knew him then surely he would know it.

The pub on the corner was packed, but he managed to struggle to the bar just before eleven. Some pubs had late opening now, but not this one. He ordered a double Scotch and a double vodka, and took them carefully away from the bar before pouring one into the other and gulping the mixture like wine. A cold fire spread through his gut, lighting him inside but making the pub seem darker. An old drunk stumbled into him and backed away, raising his hands in apology. Jason stared at the ruined face, the swollen red nose.

Too few and far between to be connected any other way.

Back at the house, he unlocked the door to the box room. Dust was smeared over the cases and boxes he'd shut away here. The grey carpet was littered with mouse turds like tiny black commas, punctuating a story he didn't want to read. Any suitcase he opened might release blind memories on tattered wings, flying around his head. Just as the fear reached a point where he'd have to curl up and hide his face, the light glinted on the rusty lock of a black briefcase.

He'd long since lost the key, but his claw hammer ripped away the leather flap easily. With the hammer still in one hand, he reached inside and took out the small gun and the clip of bullets. Never used – at least, not on something alive. He lifted it to his mouth, kissed the side of the barrel.

That night, he slept with the loaded gun on the bedside table. He'd find a quiet place to test it. As sleep wove its cobwebs against his face, pulling him down into a stillness where no memory could find him, Jason whispered an old verse silently to himself. He had no idea what it meant. But then, it had never been anything but nonsense:

> *Far and few, far and few,*
> *Are the lands where the Jumblies live;*
> *Their heads are green, and their hands are blue,*
> *And they went to sea in a Sieve.*

Near midnight, the canal was deserted. The moonlight glinted from broken factory windows and outlined shapeless masses of weed and dead leaves on the water surface. There was no colour anywhere. Jason made his way cautiously down the slope from the trees opposite the Yardley cemetery, then followed the barely visible towpath towards Digbeth and the city centre. Across the dull water, the backs of derelict factories were coated with mould. The night air was so cold you had to breathe it in before it released its smell of decay.

The last time he'd been down here, there'd been narrowboats on the water and lights in the factory windows. A generation ago – but he'd made no children to grow up, and neither had Clare. They'd walked this way together, as far as the old church at Bordesley Green. Where the fencing gave way to a cluster of workshops and brickyards, easy to break into from the canal side.

Ahead of him, the city lights hung like a dripping constellation. He thought he could see a faint red light among them, making its way towards him. The gun was a hard weight against his ribs. It had to be Danny Vail – but why had he waited so long? Like water in a barrel, accumulating worms and decay before it finally overflowed.

He'd always been mad. A little pale-faced Jewish boy with a hook nose they'd teased him about, called him 'Dong' after the Edward Lear poem they'd read in first year. The Dong with the luminous nose. But Clare had liked him, and had relieved him of his virginity before deciding she needed something harder. He'd broken up with her when she joined the Yardbirds.

Jason had made a play for her, of course, and she'd gone as far as slow kissing with him in the cinema on the Coventry Road. But that was it. Tony hadn't got much further, and Mark wouldn't have dared try anything with Gail around. But Jason had got more and more obsessed with Clare. She was the boldest of the gang: the one who stole for the challenge of it, ran the most dangerous errands, got out of trouble with an innocent smile and a clean pair of heels.

He'd come to believe that the thrill of petty crime was the only kind of sex Clare was interested in. But he'd still taken every opportunity to watch her at a distance, eavesdrop on her conversations. And one night he'd seen her emerging from a garage with Terry Joiner – who was a grown-up criminal, one of a serious local gang called the Finish. When they'd gone, Jason had slipped into the unlit garage and seen the evidence. Picked up the used condom and sniffed it, jealousy pulsing through his brain like sheet lightning.

A few days later, the Yardbirds' main capital – a stash of banknotes and speed wraps worth nearly five hundred pounds – went missing. Only they knew where it had been hidden, in a builder's yard off the Grand Union Canal. Jason went to Mark and Gail, told them he'd overheard Clare talking about it with Terry. 'She said she wants to join the Finish. That was the price of her getting in. That and…

whatever else she was giving him. I saw them come out of a garage.'

The five of them walked out from the Swan Centre, on a winter night like this one. Maybe a little colder. There was ice on the black water. Clare wasn't keen to go, said she was feeling sick. Had she guessed what was coming? Jason avoided looking at her, when usually he couldn't look at anything else. They reached the unlit yard, crawled through the gap in the chain-link fence. Mark took a torch out of his shoulder bag, as usual. Then he brought out a coil of rope and a kitchen knife. Clare just stared at him.

She wouldn't talk. Denied there was anything between her and Terry. Said the Yardbirds was the only gang she'd ever wanted to belong to. Stared hard at everyone else, one by one, when Gail started talking about the missing speed and cash. 'Tie her up,' Gail said. And then the beating started. Jason felt sick and excited at the same time. It went too far, they were too young to stay in control. The knife was used. Then Clare broke and confessed to everything. How she was already in the Finish. How she'd handed Terry the stolen stuff. How she'd give the Yardbirds anything they wanted, any way they wanted, if they'd let her go.

And all the exhilaration of victory drained from them, leaving only chill and darkness, when Gail said, 'We can't.'

It was Tony who knocked her out, using one of the bricks that littered the yard. They half-filled a canvas bag with bricks and tried to put her in, but she wouldn't fit. So they tied the bag around her waist and lowered her into the canal. There was no moon that night, and Jason hadn't seen her face in the water. That hadn't stopped him seeing it since.

A few weeks later, most of the body came to the surface.

The police talked to the Yardbirds – he suspected Danny was responsible for that – but there was no evidence. How could sixteen-year-olds possibly be involved in that? More suspicion fell on the Finish, who had to clear out of the region for good. The secret broke up the Yardbirds, of course, and Jason lost touch with the others before he'd even finished school. Thirty years of nothing. And now this.

Where the chain-link fence had been, a rusty sheet of corrugated iron was lying flat on the gravel. Beyond it, he could make out a few bags of rubbish and a loose coil of razor wire. A grey rat crept out of the shadows towards Jason, then stopped. Jason pulled out the gun and fired, missing the rat. The sound echoed from the blank factory walls.

He'd bought the gun with the money from his first job, cleaning old car parts in a garage so they could be sold as scrap. It had taken him a long time to raise the money. He'd never used the cash, or sold the powder, that he'd taken from the builder's yard and hidden in the misshapen stone bridge further along the canal. For all he knew, that package was still there. That was the first real lesson he'd learned: you can never pay back.

The house was in Sparkbrook, near the ruins of the Angel pub. Nearly ten years since the tornado had blown a tree into its roof, but no sign of any repair work. Even after midnight, some of the Asian groceries on the Stratford Road were open for business. Jason had parked half a mile away to avoid being noticed. He approached the house warily, but there was no light in the windows. The front yard was heavily overgrown with brambles and shrubs. The door needed a new coat of paint. All the curtains were open.

Looking for Danny Vail on the Internet had been a long shot – and finding his name in the *Birmingham Mail* online had been a shock. He was the contact for an educational theatre company that visited schools in the Midlands. It had to be the same guy – Jason remembered he'd been keen on drama. So he hadn't been able to leave either. They'd lived within five miles of each other all this time, but Jason didn't remember seeing him since they'd left school. If he could find Danny, then Danny could find him. It was time to act.

His breaking and entering skills were rusty, but he was well prepared. Down the side alley and through the fence, smashing a few rain-blackened planks. Over the chaotic back garden to a window that hadn't been cleaned in years. Glue sprayed on the window, a bin bag stuck over the glass. A few gentle taps with a rock hammer and the glass came away like burnt skin. No sound anywhere in the house. The smell of damp and bleach. He drew the gun and walked slowly up the unlit stairs.

In the bedroom, a crumpled single bed with no occupant. There were two flattened cans on a low table. Jason twisted the catch on one. Some kind of paint, was it face-paint? There was more in the other can: one blue, the other green. Narrow fingers had left grooves in the paint.

The next room was a kind of study, with bookshelves and an old wooden desk that even had an inkwell. The walls were covered with sheets of paper. Jason moved his torch-beam over a few of them. They were photocopies of pages from old books – Edward Lear, Lewis Carroll, others he didn't recognise. Nonsense poems with grotesque Victorian illustrations. The books on the shelves were all children's books, fifty or more years old. They smelt faintly of decay.

One book was lying on the desk, face down. An antique copy of Lear's collected poems. Jason sat down and put the loaded gun by his right hand. Then he opened the book. A thin scrap of paper fell out. A cigarette paper, with something written on it in tiny old-fashioned script. He had to hold it against the back cover of the book to make out the words:

> *There was a young lady named Clare*
> *Who died with green weed in her hair*
> *And her hands that were still*
> *Turned blue from the chill*
> *Alas, there was no one to care*

Was that someone moving downstairs, or just the sounds of an old house settling in the night? Jason switched off his torch. There was no light on the staircase. He was still holding the old book. A faint scratching sound – probably mice. Then the door swung open silently. He glimpsed a tiny skull-like face with a red light attached to it. With a dreamlike slowness, he lifted the gun. It was only as his finger curled on the trigger that he realised the barrel was pointing at his own head.

―――――――

The shot echoed in the still house. Danny thought the whole district had blown up. The intruder's face tore off like a mask, exposing the ruin behind it. The desk was coated with blood. Danny stood for a while, shaking. He'd got to phone the police. But there was something he needed to understand first. Why had the burglar been sitting in the dark? He'd known there was someone here from the shattered living room window. But the power cut had stopped him putting the light on. Instead, he'd found the face-torch that he wore for cycling after dark.

He didn't know why the intruder had shot himself. Nor could he explain the green paint in the dead man's hair or the blue paint on his hands. It looked rather like the make-up he'd been using for the new children's show. Could this be one of his colleagues? He couldn't recognise what was left of the face. And despite the horror of the situation, he was conscious of real anger. The madman had got blood all over his book. His special book – the one he'd read aloud from every night for thirty years, as if it were a book of prayers or spells.

FEELS LIKE UNDERGROUND

WITH CHRIS MORGAN

It was the coldest morning so far this winter. The clouds had blurred into a whitish gauze, through which the sunlight glittered like patches of frost. At first, he'd thought the car would never start. Then he'd lost an hour queuing behind lorries and buses on the Warwick Road, where the open-plan traffic system seemed to induce a kind of collective paranoia. It wasn't until he got past Solihull, and the landscape opened out into soft fields and perspiring woodland, that Mark began to think about the conference ahead. Two days of market-speak, management-speak, the voice of the corporate sphincter. Two days of spreadsheets, SWOT analyses, performance indicators, outside-the-box thinking, acetates and acronyms. Two days of Brian's cigars and Graham's nervous jokes. Two nights with Cathy.

The hotel was near a village called Wormleighton, out in the extensively franchised wilds of rural Warwickshire. It was called The Pines. According to Graham, who'd stayed there for a conference in 1993, it had a kind of Swiss/Austrian feel. 'Sort of a Black Forest château.' In his conference folder, Mark had a leaflet about the hotel. It showed a murky, faux-Gothic building, surrounded by fir trees. There was a small lake to one side, probably artificial. The leaflet ended with the words: *You'll be pining to return.* Cathy had said it reminded her of a Leadbelly song about jealousy, about a murdered husband. Mark hadn't known what to say to that.

Cathy was the human resources manager at the Bromsgrove site. Mark was a production manager at the Knowle site. They'd met at a sales conference the previous year, and again at the Neotechnic Christmas party. Which was where the affair had started, really, though they hadn't slept together until a hastily arranged night just before the New Year. It wasn't just the need for discretion that made him cautious. Mark didn't want to get in so deep he couldn't get out again. Cathy understood. Her marriage was a lot shakier than his; but even so, she wasn't the kind to take risks. It had to be kept on ice, like a bottle of vodka you were saving for a special occasion. Still, he'd been looking forward to this weekend in an increasingly obsessive manner over the last couple of weeks. Whatever the room arrangements were, they'd find a way to be together. She'd promised that, in an almost tearful mid-evening call from her office to his. A call that had ended with them listening to each other's breath, as if they were falling asleep in the same bed.

The sketch map in the conference folder showed a narrow road going through Wormleighton, then uphill to the small forest around the hotel. Mark saw a grey stone tower, then a partly ruined manor house. He glanced at the fields, seeing horses, cattle and, unexpectedly, a chestnut-coated stag. Jackdaws circled in pairs above the trees. The roadway was smeared with frost. He slowed down, unsure of the route. A flash of sunlight melted the windscreen, dazzling him. Cathy floated behind his vision. Her short auburn hair, cut in a high fringe at the back. Her upturned nose. Her beautiful smile, the teeth just a little too strong. Her dark, painful eyes. Mark shook his head, banishing the image. The road was lined with trees now: firs, cedars, pines. Almost the only green things left in January. Winter felt like an absence, not a season at all.

Suddenly, the view to one side fell away. A small lake was set in the hillside. Almost circular, frozen. It must be far colder here than in the city. The ice was marked with blotches of white. Two kids were skating on it. Mark slowed down to watch them. A boy and a girl, about fifteen, similarly dressed in ski jackets and black jeans. Their linked hands were ungloved. It was like the slow dance at the end of a disco. He felt like a voyeur; but it was hard to look away. The car stopped, braked. The couple moved together, spiralling outward in a shared arc. They kissed. Mark was suddenly aware of the frozen mass that held them up. The coldness that freed them to move and touch. He turned the key in the ignition and drove on.

Half a mile further, the road widened into a car park. The hotel was there: dark, angular, unexpectedly small. Most of its windows were shuttered. There were traces of snow on the surrounding trees, though he'd not seen any driving up here. As he got out of the car, the sunlight flared like burning plastic. Cold air scratched at his face. As he pulled his suitcase out of the boot, he realised he was crying. Quickly he wiped his eyes, hoping no one had seen him. Red eyes wouldn't look good at the conference: they'd think he'd been drinking. Around the car park, various familiar suits were getting out of burnished company cars. Without greeting any of them, Mark straightened his tie and walked into the hotel.

The interior was lit entirely by candles, high up in multi-armed candlesticks around the lobby and the staircase. Red velvet awnings and black furniture gave it a vaguely gothic feel, like the set of a Roger Corman film. However, the message board used modern lettering. He gathered that the first seminar was in the Holst Room, followed by lunch in the Beethoven Suite. Mark's room was on the second floor. He decided to use the staircase, which looked like marble: a pearly white veined with crimson. The steps were too large, and slightly damp; when he grasped the handrail, its surface was greasy with polish. The effort of climbing made him worry about his fitness. Too much driving, not enough exercise. On the first-floor landing, he glanced upward through the long matrix of the staircase: a tight coil around darkness, like a fossil of some primitive organism.

Reception had warned him about the electricity in his room. You had to use the door key to connect it – unlocking the light, so to speak, before pressing the switch. The wavering candlelight from the corridor hardly diluted the shadows in the room. He fumbled inside the door, smelling dust and wax polish. Then the light sprang on: two yellow lamps in wall brackets, neither more than forty watts. If he needed to work in here, he'd complain. There was a low but comfortable-looking bed, with a red velvet bedspread and two black pillows. He lay back on it, suddenly aroused by the thought of Cathy. Would she be at the first seminar? Forcing himself to think about work, he sat up and blinked at the wall. There was a picture of a forest, black distorted trees against a murky sunset. Or was it a fire?

Unpacking only what he needed for the seminar, Mark hurried back down the precarious steps to the ground floor. The Holst Room was probably as close to a normal conference room as this place got. Long, curved tables formed shells around a space at the back, where an OHP had been set up next to an old-fashioned lectern. The first few rows were full already. Mark nodded and smiled at a few colleagues; then he sat near the back, looking out for Cathy. No sign. During the next two hours, while the three sales directors droned on about marketing strategies and the audience laughed politely in what they guessed were the right places, Mark's imagination kept returning to the black-sheeted bed. He took notes dutifully, sketching cats and spiders in the wide margins. At least this room had electric lights. The final Q&A session dragged, sales colleagues asking for information they already had just to show off how well-researched the department was.

The Beethoven Suite was at the end of a long corridor whose walls were panelled in mahogany. The light from stainless steel candelabras glittered on crystal glasses and etiolated cutlery. It was a very quiet room, probably soundproofed, though some low music vibrated from the floor. There was a buffet and carvery on the far side of the room. Just inside the door, a grand piano stood in dust-free silence. Mark wondered if it was an injection-moulded replica. As he joined the queue, a hand brushed his arm. 'Hi there.'

For a moment, he almost reached out to hold her. The candles flickered, sending out a ripple of darkness. Then he recovered. 'Cathy! How long have you been here?' It was getting harder to cover up in front of colleagues.

'About an hour,' she said. 'Some motorway trouble. An accident just in front of me. They took down my name and address, as a witness. One driver had to go to hospital. Then I got here... and got stuck in the lift. My room's on the fifth floor.' Mark felt a twinge of disappointment. 'Must have pressed the wrong button coming down. The lift door opened, and there was just this wall. Brick and plaster. No light outside the lift. I could hear something. Like... wax. Dripping.' She looked away. 'I kept pressing buttons, but nothing happened. It was *cold* down there. I thought... then something connected and the lift shot back up to this floor. By the time I'd recovered and made a complaint to Reception, the seminar was due to finish.'

Cathy was shivering. Mark squeezed her arm gently. 'I'm okay,' she said. Her smile made him feel breathless. *Be careful,* he thought. *This is dangerous.* For a moment, absurdly, he couldn't remember his wife's name.

The afternoon was slightly less dull than the morning. One of Cathy's colleagues from the bright lights of Bromsgrove led an imaginative (if slightly insincere) discussion on risk-taking in business management. Later, Mark gave a report on production control methods in the Glass Suite, a sparsely furnished room decorated with repetitive abstract motifs on tiny pieces of acetate. His small audience was too busy taking notes to appreciate any of the jokes – which was reassuring for Mark, since they didn't seem funny to him either. Especially the comment about how mobile phones, like their vectors, were dropping in price.

Then there was a break, during which he and Cathy slipped out for a quiet walk. It was unexpectedly cold; neither of them had an overcoat. Darkness was gathering in the trees, filtering down from the burnt sky. No one was skating on the lake; deep cracks ran across the ice, though not deep enough to expose the water. After checking that they were alone, Mark slipped his arms around Cathy and kissed her deeply. They rocked together, listening to the silence. Cathy's jacket rode up as she embraced him, the shoulder-pads trembling like vestigial wings. Without speaking, they returned to the hotel.

The final session before dinner was a report on the ways Neotechnic was developing its use of IT resources. There were four speakers, including Cathy. She talked about how the company used its intranet for communications. 'Of course, a website has no real privacy. Rivals can hack into it if they want to. So the information is only confidential if it's information that no one wants. For secrets, use the phone. For *real* secrets...' Cathy bent down and whispered something into Brian's ear. Mark felt an irrational surge of jealousy. *Lighten up,* he thought. Cathy glanced at him and smiled; he didn't manage to smile back.

Feeling angry with himself, and uneasy at the way things seemed to be slipping, Mark went up to his room to unpack before dinner. This time he took the lift, and almost went flying when he stepped out into a corridor whose floor was about six inches below the lift's. He limped to his room, unlocked the door and the light, and wondered whether the smell of wax came from the furniture polish or the candles in the hallway. There was a small chest of drawers by the bed; the top drawer at first refused to budge, then shot clean out from its runners, banging Mark's knuckles and just missing his legs. Reciting a list of obscure sexual practices, he replaced the drawer and put some underwear in it. Then he hung up his jacket in a wardrobe tall enough for suicide.

Familiar with hotel showers, Mark adjusted the temperature control before turning on the water. The resulting blast made him think of steam trains. Biting his lip, he turned down the temperature until the water abruptly turned lukewarm. There was no reduction in the force of the spray. The shower cubicle's floor was smooth, not unlike the stairs, and became dangerous when coated with soapy water. When he stepped out of the cubicle, rubbing his eyes, Mark discovered that the shower had leaked heavily onto the bathroom floor. He dried his feet while sitting on the bed. It was tempting to lie down and think about Cathy. But that could wait. He wouldn't need to dream later. And he'd better get his feelings under control before rejoining the others.

Almost as an afterthought, he phoned Linda at home. The connection was faulty; as she talked about their son, Mark heard snow falling through the line into his head. 'Those computer games we had to get him for Christmas – he hasn't touched them all week. Whenever he gets excited about something new, he thinks it's going to matter for the rest of his life. And then a few weeks later, it's completely forgotten. He outgrows things, but he doesn't seem to outgrow… the mentality.' *Or the need,* Mark thought with a twinge of bitterness. He said something non-committal about Dominic having time to change. He was only nine.

'That's the problem,' Linda said. 'These advertisers, they're destroying time. They're franchising childhood. It's not a part of life any more, it's a market.' As usual, Mark found himself both agreeing with her viewpoint and concerned about her state of mind. There was no sense in being an outsider. Linda's anger helped to give him a sense of purpose; but he still had to fit in, had to be part of the system. Did that make him a hypocrite? One more thing to feel guilty about.

———

There was a draught in the stairwell; Mark shivered as he negotiated the whitish steps. Graham was standing in the foyer, wearing a horrible mauve tie. 'Mark! Come and join the party. You need to join something.' Mark followed him into the Brahms Suite, which turned out to be the bar. He downed a quick vodka and orange, trying to identify Cathy among the gleaming men and power-dressed women. Someone leaned back into the outer corner of a dado rail and cried out, 'God! What's that doing there?' Tall candles flickered in brass rosettes all around. 'There's something dangerous about this place...' concluded the speaker. *You don't know the half of it,* Mark thought. He shut his eyes and saw drifting squares of light crossing a blue surface: the Windows screen saver.

'Are you okay?' It was Brian, wearing a crimson silk shirt and looking concerned. Mark nodded and swallowed the last of his drink. The vodka felt colder inside him than the ice cubes. He made for the Gents sign at the corner of the bar. It was dim and quiet in these; the piped music, presumably either Brahms or Liszt, was more clearly audible. He splashed water over his face and blinked repeatedly. The window-images wouldn't go away. Like flaws in a sheet of ice. He wondered exactly what Graham had meant about joining something. It could have been a coded reference to the staff Christmas party, when Mark had spent the whole evening talking with Cathy and ignored the various bonding rituals going on within his department. Or it could have had something to do with Mark's lack of enthusiasm for the major political parties. The politics of his colleagues repelled him: both the ingrained Conservatism of the directors and the shallow opportunism of those managers who'd switched their allegiance from the ghost of Thatcher to the hologram of Blair. As if all that mattered was identifying and following the highest achiever.

His reverie was broken by the coughing of an elderly military-looking man in a yellow jacket. 'They ought to change the mirrors in this place,' the stranger muttered. 'Whenever I look at one, I don't like what I see.' Mark smiled in what he hoped was a supportive fashion. It hadn't occurred to him that there might be permanent residents in this hotel. He went back to the bar, where Cathy was waiting in a turquoise blouse and skirt that made the candlelight back off in astonishment. 'Is your room comfortable?' she asked him, smiling. Her eyes were serious, almost frightened.

They ate in a different function room from lunch. Mark didn't see the name, but assumed it to be the Wagner Suite from the décor, which included plastic mountain peaks moulded onto the walls and a glittering silvery waterfall running into a trench at one end of the room. The ceiling was painted with a fluorescent aurora borealis. Large red candles melted over the wall surface, turning mountains to volcanoes and burning small mahogany villages. They drank some rich Austrian red wine and ate a mixture of game that included rabbit. The music periodically drowned out conversation. Which, given that the conversation on both sides of Mark seemed to revolve around current trends in the business-related software market, was no great loss. Cathy was sitting nearly opposite him, too far away for their legs to touch. Their eyes brushed across each other every few minutes, caressing without holding. She rarely wore lipstick, but tonight her mouth was very slightly reddened. Or maybe it was just the wine and the flickering light.

Later, the gathering divided itself between several rooms. Most of the older staff settled in the Brahms Suite for a quiet drinking session. Mark decided to stay as sober as possible. Once he got past a certain point with wine or spirits, he lost the ability to stop. At one level, he wanted to drink until the conflicting voices of lust and fear dissolved into a bright silence. At another level, he knew that would be a criminal waste. He joined Cathy in the Saint-Saëns Room, where a retrogressive disco was in progress. The sight of young executives reliving their teens, strutting and weaving to the sounds of Blondie and Donna Summer, made him feel uneasy. You could play the same records all your life, but it was frightening how soon you forgot the moves. The room was oppressively dark and warm, with red velvet curtains and a black tiled floor.

After a quick trip back to the bar, Mark and Cathy went on to the Zann Room, where the younger staff seemed to have gathered. The music here was louder and distinctly atonal, a blend of techno and trip-hop that shuddered with confusion. Nobody was dancing very much. The walls were blue-grey, pricked with thousands of tiny lights like strange drifting constellations. Mark recognised Gary and Sue from the IT department; they were kissing slowly, their faces blurred by the moving lights. Sue waved at him and said something, but he couldn't hear her voice. He felt Cathy's hand on his arm, turned to see her mouth framing silent words. He reached up and touched her hair. They stood like that for a moment. Then Cathy smiled, tugged his sleeve and led him out into the corridor.

They would have gone up the stairs together, but someone was lurking in the stairwell, watching the entrance. It was Brian. 'Hi,' he said in a childlike voice. 'Feel a bit woozy. Too much red wine. Thought I might get an early night.' He leaned on the banister, still gazing at the main doorway. Brian wasn't a drinker, Mark recalled. Maybe he'd broken his own rules. Cathy and Mark wandered awkwardly back to the Saint-Saëns Room, which was becoming crowded. On little tables around the floor, glasses jittered to the pedestrian beat of 'Life in the Fast Lane'. The smells of perfume, burnt wax and spilt wine stiffened the air.

When it happened, it seemed like the room had been waiting for it. One of the heavier executives slipped on the tiled floor, staggered and fell. A woman grabbed at his arm, but missed and fell over him, her feet trapped under his jacket. Her pale wrist snapped with a sound like breaking ice. There was a brief silence. Then her shocked face released a thin cry, as if she wanted to scream but couldn't. Her right hand flopped like a glove until she gripped and straightened it.

The man on the floor sat up, breathless but apparently unhurt. One by one, the other dancers stopped moving.

Another woman knelt by the casualty, spoke to her and helped her to her feet. Before the record had finished playing, two uniformed hotel employees came through a side door and led the injured woman away in a slow procession. Obviously someone would take her to the hospital – which might be as far away as Leamington. Mark didn't know who she was.

'They should have stopped the music,' Cathy said. They were climbing the stairs together, Brian having disappeared. It was nearly midnight. 'No one was moving, the DJ must have known there'd been an accident even if he didn't see it. Why didn't he turn the record off?' Mark didn't answer. Each step felt like a hurdle between himself and Cathy. The lift would have been quicker and more discreet; but after Cathy's experience this morning, it didn't seem worth the risk. On the second floor, they paused. 'Your room okay?' Mark nodded. He was glad of the alcohol, which was taking the edge off his panic. Under the soft fleshy glow of the wine, he felt like he'd been stuffed with darkness. The link between himself and his life outside was nothing more than a telephone line. He'd lost the code.

They were alone. Mark unlocked his door and reached for the light-switch before remembering to use his key. Cathy stood while he shut the door and hung up his jacket. In the dim light, he could only see vague patches of colour: the red bedspread, blue-green wallpaper, yellow lamps. The only sound in the room was their breathing. He put his arms around Cathy's waist and drew her against him. Her tongue was thin and soft, dancing in his mouth. He stroked her hair, running his fingers down to the back of her neck. *You're beautiful*, he whispered to her. Cathy looked down. *Don't say anything,* she whispered back. *Not now.* She was unbuttoning his shirt, her fingernails pricking his chest. He kissed her neck, feeling the pulse just under the white skin.

Naked, they pulled back the bedspread and climbed onto the taut black sheet, then folded themselves around each other. The combination of black and red made him think suddenly of the Neotechnic logo. In the poor light Cathy's eyes were opaque, somehow lifeless. But her teeth glistened, and he could see the faint blush on her throat and collarbone. He reached between her legs and touched what felt like a skinless muscle. The air was chilly, but they were both sweating. The surface of the bed was firm. Cathy gripped his penis and guided him into her, closing tight around him. Her fingernails drew tracks across his shoulder blades. After a few minutes, she pulled back and twisted over so that he could enter her from behind. Mark pressed the palms of his hands against her nipples and kissed the thin curve of her right ear. They were facing into the room by now, the pillows forgotten. A flicker of light on the wall made him look up. It was the forest painting. The sunset was moving through the trees, setting them on fire. The wallpaper seemed to ripple and flow like a tidal sea. The twin lamps stuttered their dirty light. Below him, Cathy shuddered as her cry broke into gasps. The wall was coming. The room was coming. He thrust deep and then held still, feeling the darkness inside him melt and escape.

It was only then that he realised he wasn't wearing a condom. Those risks weren't part of the plan. What was wrong with him? They disengaged and lay still for a while, in an uneasy silence. Mark wondered if the blind violence of their lovemaking was a distorted expression of their growing depth of feeling. If so, it was a sign that things were getting out of control. As their bodies cooled, a chill seemed to rise through the mattress and drive them back together. Half covered by the velvet bedspread, they embraced and murmured tenderly until they were ready to make love again. This time, it was gentler and more human; they cried each other's names as their bodies crumpled together. Afterward, Mark lay awake in the darkness, wondering why the first time had been so much better. Maybe love needed some coolness to protect it. Fire and ice. *You're pissed,* he thought with some bitterness. Cathy had set the alarm for eight.

During the night, the fire alarm went off. Naked and shivering, Mark walked down a flight of concrete steps and along a blank whitewashed corridor. The fire escape presumably led out the back of the hotel, but there were voices all around him. Everyone must have gathered down here. Cathy had gone ahead of him. After a while, he came to an open doorway through which pale lights flickered. There was an intense smell of melting wax. The voices were crying out, but not in pain. He stepped through the doorway and was trapped in folds of dark cloth.

The digital alarm clock ticked softly, like a dripping candle. It was nearly four o'clock. Mark was painfully aroused, but he'd have to wait until morning. Cathy was stretched beside him, her breathing only just audible. Suddenly his mind lit up with images of the basement. Ringed by the remains of candles, the dozens of writhing bodies. Scraps of underwear crumpled on hands and faces. Reddened skin, marked with circles of wax and semen. A little furtively, he gripped his cock; but the images faded at once, leaving him confused and hollow. The dream reminded him of something he'd always imagined at company meetings: that wherever you got to in the hierarchy, there was some kind of inner circle you couldn't reach. The real party was the one you were not invited to. The air in the bedroom was cool and smelt only of furniture polish, as if cleaners had come in the night and erased the residues of lovemaking. Mark tried to replay their desperate coupling of a few hours before; but it seemed facile, staged, like glossy soft porn. He closed his eyes against the darkness and tried to float back into sleep.

It didn't work. A couple of hours later, his curiosity got the better of him. Moving as quietly as possible, he switched on the bedside lamp and put his clothes on, apart from his shoes and jacket. He closed the door carefully behind him and padded along the half-lit corridor to where he'd dreamt the fire escape to be. It was there; he must have seen it earlier. The door opened on a spring and closed silently when he released it. A long flight of concrete steps, going down into the heart of the building. The chill numbed his feet and made walking difficult. Some faint light, possibly moonlight, filtered down from above. The air was damp and still, like some rotten fabric he had to tear through to reach his destination.

At the foot of the stairs was an unlit corridor. He could feel paint on one of the side walls. The texture was soft and crumbly. There were no side doors. He thought the floor was damp, though there was hardly any sensation in his feet. Near the opening at the end of the corridor, he paused. There was no sound. He walked through, conscious of a growing sexual excitement. Another staircase, completely invisible. He thought the steps were metal, and not entirely solid. Another passage, hardly wide enough to walk through. He could hear the very faint sound of dripping, as regular as a clock. The passage ended in a brick wall. Unless he'd missed it, there was no side exit. The fire escape was a dead end. He pressed his hands to the moist stone, bewildered by its refusal to yield. Suddenly all he wanted was to be asleep in bed.

It took him a while to get back, climbing stairs that felt uneven as well as steep. The sound of dripping faded above the basement level, and the silence frightened him. Eventually he stumbled through the doorway onto the second floor. It was daylight. His feet and the palms of his hands were black with dust. As he turned towards the corridor, a swing door opened. It was Brian and a teenage boy he'd not seen before. Feeling vaguely reassured, Mark crept back to his room and let himself in. The heavy curtains kept in the night. He undressed quietly and got into bed beside Cathy, who was still asleep. As his head touched the pillow, the alarm clock went off.

Breakfast was edgy and subdued. From the number of blank faces and dropped-shadow eyes at the table in the Stravinsky Suite, Mark suspected he'd not been the only one to have trouble sleeping. The unnatural dawn chorus of stringed instruments playing throughout the room jarred his nerves. Too lively for winter. He learned that Tara from marketing, who'd broken her arm the night before, had stayed in hospital overnight and was going home today. That hadn't been the only accident: Ian the accounts manager was limping after a fall in the shower. The left side of his face was bruised grey, like a school playground after rain.

The opening session was a workshop on time management, which overran by half an hour. The two seminars ran concurrently: Graham on what the company could learn from Japanese corporate strategies, and Cathy on new trends in HR management. For professional reasons, Mark had to attend the former. It dragged, like a haiku extended into fifty-five cantos. Cathy's sleeping face drifted across his field of vision, as perfect and expressionless as a mask. It scared him, to feel so deeply about something that would never be complete. It was trapped deep inside him: not guilt and not joy, but something in between. Her fluid movements tracked fire across the inside of his skull; the way she fucked was no more and no less beautiful than the way she drank coffee or sent a fax.

Just before lunch, they slipped away together and went back to the frozen lake. Mark thought he could see a pattern of circular skate-tracks, like the groove in a record. White vinyl. Yesterday's cracks were no longer visible. They held hands, listening to the minimalist percussion of bare twigs in the wind and the random cries of seagulls that were circling above the lake. Cathy was worried about her seminar. 'Whenever I talk about *managing human resources*, it's like I've crossed a line between relating to people and using them. It's a science. Every decision I make could be made by a computer. They don't want *me*, just a machine with my voice. Because a human voice has more power to manipulate.'

Mark wanted to say something, to reassure her; but he was thinking about his own managerial routines, the way he used staff appraisals and one-on-one scheduling meetings to control the members of his department. The same rationale: it isn't *me*, it's the company. This is how things are done. No wonder he felt cheated. They kissed slowly, their fear sheathed by the cold. The ice shimmered like quartz below them.

———————

The whole afternoon was taken up by a company progress report, with several American directors in attendance. The air was thick with virtual dollar signs. Despite the company's record-breaking profits, every other directive was about cost-cutting. Mark had been working to a shoestring budget for so long, it took events like this to remind him how much money the company actually made. The managing director, a man only ever referred to by his initials, laid heavy emphasis on the significance of budgetary control. 'The key to successful expansion is effective downsizing. *We* need to be in control of the workplace culture and the workflow in our departments. *Our* culture, the *Neotechnic* culture, not anyone else's. We're all working hard to phase out union recognition throughout all branches of the company. I don't need to tell you how important that is, with the prospect of a new British government letting in socialist legislation from Europe. The unions will be desperately keen to help ministers interfere in the way we run our business. Your jobs depend on keeping a tight ship.'

Afterward, Mark stood at the foot of the staircase, gazing up into the cold white spiral and its missing heart. A rush of vertigo made him shiver. It felt like he'd been at a political rally. But it was only business. For a moment, he wanted to be free of everything. He'd wait until tomorrow before phoning Linda. His head was full of corporate rhetoric and pornographic images. It wasn't stuff he wanted to share.

That evening was quieter than the previous one. Perhaps the weighty presence of the MD and some of the

205

directors, who'd turned up for the afternoon, was creating an atmosphere of restraint. People like that wouldn't risk denting the premiums on their health insurance policies. Whatever the reason, there was no disco. A long-drawn-out meal involving smoked sausages, veal pastries and chocolate cake was followed by an hour or so of obligatory networking, then a quiet drinking session spread across three smoke-blurred bars. Mark and Brian – who'd got over his embarrassment about the dawn incident when he'd realised that Mark didn't give a fuck about it – explored the ground floor, a labyrinth of tacky function rooms connected by dark-red corridors. Some of them were showing clear signs of neglect. The Elgar Suite, right at the back of the hotel, was an enclave of British Empire memorabilia where the hotel's older residents gathered to get quietly wrecked; visitors were not welcome. The Rachmaninov Suite was locked; dust furred the inside of the glass-paned door. From the dark interior, the restless sound of piano chords was just audible. The Cage Room was another bar, silent and empty apart from an effigy tipping an empty glass above its mouth.

Towards midnight, as the remaining drinkers were painting their inner landscapes with stars, Mark left Brian half-asleep in the Tchaikovsky Suite and went up to his room. There was a small plastic kettle with some sachets of instant coffee; he made a cup and drank it black, trying to sober up before Cathy arrived. He'd not seen her since dinner, when they'd arranged to meet here. After last night, the room seemed gloomy and impersonal, the forest picture unconvincing. Maybe none of it worked when you were alone. Was that why he'd been unable to find the cellar? He was still thinking about that when he heard a light, rapid series of knocks. He let her in, flicking the catch on the door as it snapped shut.

They sat together on the bed, holding each other as if any movement would risk separation. His hands moved slowly over her back and shoulders. Mark felt hollow with need. He suspected that if tonight didn't work out, they might finish. But talking about the future would only depress them both, strangling desire and isolating them in their separate rooms of guilt. It seemed like the only way forward was to fuck each other into an oblivion where anything could be said. To burn down the forest. *You're beautiful,* he whispered again. Cathy smiled. Her eyes widened, then closed as their mouths clasped together. He caressed her through her dress, trying to draw the naked Cathy out of the clothed one.

When they were lying on the velvet bedspread, she used her arms and legs to lift him clear above her, then slowly let him fall until his penis touched the smooth skin of her belly. He came within seconds of entering her, but carried on until she gasped and dug her nails into his sides. Once again, he realised, they hadn't taken precautions. The images of his dream returned; he lifted above her and letting her stroke him until his semen was tracked across her pale skin. Then he pressed his face between her legs and probed with his tongue, pushing her knees up over his tense shoulders. They went on like this for some considerable time, until they were dry and narcotised with ecstasy and the sheets were a crumpled mess. Then they pulled the duvet over themselves and slept back to back, not touching.

It was still dark when the fire alarm woke him. He sat up and listened to its echoes dying in his head. The room was chilly and almost silent: the clock ticking on one side of him, Cathy breathing softly on the other. The truth was lodged in his head, as clear as ice. How it all fitted together: the company, Cathy, the hotel. *None of it worked when you were alone.* With Cathy, he could get into the basement. What happened there would mean he could keep her. He listened to her breathing. It was too shallow and uneven for sleep. 'Cathy.'

'Yes? Mark?' There must have been a trace of moonlight in the room, since he could just make out the blurred shape of her head rising from the pillow. 'What is it?'

'The fire escape,' he said. 'You must come with me. Please? You know what I'm asking. The party. The real party. You *know*.'

There was a pause. Then she said: 'All right.' She reached out and touched his face. They kissed, invisible like ghosts. Leaving the door open, they walked naked along the corridor to the whitewashed door opposite the lift shaft. The stone steps were clammy, roughened by flakes of paint. Cathy put her arm around Mark's waist as they passed into the total darkness of the corridor, and down the flight of braided metal steps. At the bottom, Mark paused. The floor was slippery with dried wax. There was a dim light at the end of the passage, flickering. As they walked on, he could hear the sounds from the room beyond. He slipped a hand across Cathy's breasts. Her nipples were hard; she turned to kiss him. They walked together through the stone-framed doorway. There was no door.

It was a long, shallow room, roughly oval in shape, like one of the conference rooms upstairs. The centre of the room was filled with candles. More candles, in various tones of off-white and pink, hung on crude wire chandeliers from the low ceiling. Their wax had formed into the shapes of many interlinked bodies, some more complete than others. Hundreds of tiny flames winked and smouldered in the gloom; but there was no heat. The room was so cold that Cathy's breath clouded in front of her face. She stepped away from Mark, towards the edge of the many-limbed composite statue. Part of it reached out and gripped her ankle. She knelt and let the pale, waxy hand move slowly up her thigh.

Mark glanced around helplessly. More wax figures were clustered around the edge of the room, embedded in the wall or each other. He could still hear the sounds of rhythmical kissing and slapping, the moans and gasps of throats working in passion. But the only movement he could see was far too slow; and the only faces were blank screens, their eyes and mouths stopped with wax. Cathy was half-sitting now, her back curved, hands and feet dug into the mound of rippling flesh. A thick white candle was pressing between her thighs. Her eyes opened momentarily and she saw Mark. 'Join us. Don't be a stranger.' Then she twisted away and shuddered through the build-up of a violent climax. Mark watched, unable to react, as her legs kicked in the air and her right ankle broke like the stem of a glass.

He tried to reach her, but she was near the focus of the party and there were too many bodies in the way. Soon it ceased to matter, as hands and mouths fastened upon him and he was no longer alone. At last he realised, not only that the candles were people, but that the people were candles. The closer he got to them, the more human they were and the brighter they shone. However cold it might be, the party would go on. And it was freezing: he could see icicles in the dark ceiling, feel the crystals of ice on the yearning faces. A weight of flesh on his arm tore the muscle, but he felt no pain. A drifting membrane brought him to climax and he ejaculated without pleasure, watching his semen freeze in the air. Someone cried out, and the rest imitated. Mark heard his own voice among them. The image of order and repetition grew in his mind. Like a spreadsheet. A spread sheet. Living in the ice, while the dance continued overhead.

UPON A GRANITE WIND

DEDICATED TO ROBERT E. HOWARD

When I was a child we lived in a tower block on the edge of the city. One of our neighbours was an old man who'd fought in the Second World War. He'd spent two years in a German prisoner-of-war camp. One winter he stopped coming out of his flat, didn't answer the door. Eventually someone from the council broke in and there was nobody there. So they cleared out the flat and rented it to a couple. Their first night in the flat, the couple noticed a bad smell coming from the bedroom wall. They moved a bookcase and found a concealed hole in the plaster. The old man was there, trapped in the space between floors, been dead for weeks. He'd tried to dig a tunnel out of the tower block.

I'm not sure when I started to dream of the ruined city. A nervous child, I rarely slept well and was troubled by nocturnal sounds: dogs barking, drunks singing, neighbours fighting or making love. There seemed so much anger in the adult world. Glimpses of broken stone and twisted metal, houses torn open to the night, drifted through my sweating head as I covered it with a pillow. I hoarded the visions of ruin to get me through the days in a world that seemed incomprehensible and terrifying.

There was a patch of wasteground I walked across on my way home from school. A few kids always hung around there, looking for trouble. One of them was a pale-faced boy who latched on to me as being some kind of offence to his sensibility. I was a nervous child with a high-pitched voice; he used to follow me around, flapping his hands and shrieking wordless mocking nonsense. One day in winter, the sky already dark, I walked home with the boy capering one step behind me. When finally I closed the door on him, I took off my coat to find the back coated with spit. I never wore the coat again. My parents must have thrown it away. All that night I lay awake, twisting with rage and shame, visions of the ruined city denied to me.

After that, my dreams changed. The ruined city was no longer a constellation of fragments but a coherent landscape across which I ran, fought and slew. I took on robber gangs, brutal soldiers, stray beasts. Always I fought alone. The episodes seemed connected, but the city was never the same twice, and I was rarely the same man. What linked them was the legend of a solitary avenger. I would dream a savage fight, then dream of someone to whom that fight was a rumour and an inspiration. The city in its slow decay bore the marks of my lonely war: lives I had saved, graves I had filled, places scarred and stained by violence.

A world so mapped by consequences couldn't be anything but real. I soon accepted that the dreams were memories, and that I had lived many lives before this one. What they had to teach me would no doubt become clear in time. I had my share of fights in the waking world, but rarely distinguished myself. What spurred me wasn't courage, only a blind impulse to lash out at anyone who insulted me. Thereby, of course, encouraging them to add injury to insult. Through my waking life, the shadow of the mocking follower pursued me: always at a distance, never in my line of sight. He was there in my past lives too, but was no easier to reach in the ruined city – whose inexorable decay my exploits seemed unable to halt.

One night in my mid-teens, I heard voices calling to me from the street below. What name they called me by I don't remember, only that they were female voices taut with fear and longing. I pushed open the shutter and climbed down to the scarred roadway. Three painfully thin maidens were waiting for me, their faces dead white above their ragged clothing. As their hands reached out towards me, I saw the fingers were abnormally long and pale. They tugged at my sleeves, drawing me with them between the damaged buildings towards the bare, stunted trees of a wasteground.

The girls shivered, drawing closer to me. I felt no heat from their bodies. We walked through the trees to a concealed building: a small house overgrown with black moss and trailing bindweed, its windows shuttered. They led me onward to a patch of marshy ground that flickered with traces of pale blue flame. In the muddy soil I glimpsed twisted limbs, a broken spine, a face without eyes. The three ghostly maidens clustered around me, their soft fingers drawing patterns on my skin. Their voices twined into a single cry of loss.

The shock of pleasure woke me, alone in my narrow bed. Through the window frame, a draught made the curtains shiver. I felt sick. It was years before I returned to that time and that self, and saw the black house and the wasteground again. They were years in which I felt choked with helplessness. My parents divorced bitterly, my sister married a violent man with no trace of courage, and I struggled with poor health and the impulse to withdraw from everything. I had no money, but dreams are free.

Then, one winter night in my lonely bedsit, I turned a street corner and was back at the edge of the ruined city. Ahead of me was the fringe of bare trees. A ragged boy told me the legend of the sorcerer in the sealed black house. He'd not been seen in many years, but three local girls had disappeared and it was believed that he'd taken them. He drowned them in the swamp behind his house, where nobody dared go. On moonless nights he revived them for his service. The local children all knew this to be true.

Through the trees, a bitter wind carried the odour of the marsh. I paced around the low building, looking for a way to break in. The door and windows were crusted with black moss and dripping weeds. Surely nobody could live here? But through a crack in a shutter, I saw the flicker of a candle. With my dagger's edge, I prised the shutter away from the window frame and peered inside. The smoky flame revealed a tiny figure bent over a desk, his head on his arms, a huge book open before him. As I jumped in through the window, the sorcerer awoke and turned to face me.

At some dim level, my dream-self knew him: it was the boy who'd spat on me, but shrunken and bent with age. His wrinkled face twisted in mockery as he rose to mimic my stance, holding an imaginary dagger in a hand that he flapped from a limp wrist. Losing control, I charged at him. He backed into a corner and chanted a phrase in a language I didn't know. His gaunt fingers wove shapes from the air, like flattened birds with long black tails and fanged beaks. They flew around my head, wheeling and striking even as I stabbed at them. Their blood faded like smoke, but mine ran thickly into my eyes and mouth. Through a shimmering red veil I saw the magician capering and sneering a mere yard away, beyond my reach.

My bloodstained hand fell to his desk, touching the open book. I could see it was of brittle parchment, the pages written in red ink. Lifting the grimoire by its wooden cover, I desperately cried out the first words I saw. At once, the daemon birds wheeled above my head. The sorcerer froze where he stood, cursing me in a choked voice. For a moment I glanced around the squalid room, the dying candle revealing cobwebs and the marks of rats. Moth cocoons nearly covered the low ceiling. And he was mocking me. Resisting the urge to knock out his rotting teeth, I dragged him to the window and climbed out, pulling him after me.

Rain was falling from the unlit sky. Only the scars of blue phosphorescence on the rancid marsh let me see its pitted surface and the shape of my captive. The ground became less firm as we moved forward. In the centre of the wasteground it was probably liquid. Trapped by his own spell, the sorcerer trembled with sudden fear. His victims would make him their toy. Now I saw them rising from the black mud, heard their lonely and desperate song. His three brides reached out to him with long ghostly fingers. Other figures, more badly decayed or mutilated, waited behind them. I lifted his small body and threw it into the wet core of the marsh. He sank and rose again, his face coated with mud: blind and voiceless, like the house he'd occupied for so many years. Then he was gone, and the ghosts followed him back into the corrupt depths. I turned away from the flickering blue light and felt rain on my face.

Years passed in the waking world. I grew used to work and dating, though intimacy always seemed to lead back into the cave of isolation. In the workplace, handling the cash that others build up and let go like sand, I learned to bite my tongue at insults. My heart – both its tissue and its inner voice – paid a slow price, but I struggled on.

One moonless night I paced the streets of the ruined city, knowing a fresh shadow hung over its dwindling population. Horror had struck four times in a week. Each time, a lumbering, barely human shape had snatched a young girl, crushing or rending anyone who stood in its way. A trail of shapeless, murky prints led to the swamp behind the black house in the trees.

They said the creature was three hands taller than a man, and strong enough to rip a door from its fastenings. When a dagger stabbed its rancid flesh, it did not bleed or falter – nor did the attacker have a second chance. Those it killed were smeared with grey foulness. Those it bore away – nobody liked to think.

The city's soldiers were in another land, fighting some interminable and costly war. As I walked, other figures slipped from houses and alleys to make their way, wearily yet with determination, towards the market square. There, with no formal leader, more than fifty people had gathered. The empty stalls gleamed with rain. By the light of flickering lanterns that gave our shadows fever, we stood and talked urgently.

The priests had called for a human sacrifice to appease the city's disappointed gods. Men spoke with doubt and anger of the plan. 'We have lost enough daughters.' There were young maidens in the assembly, perhaps safer there than left at home. A thought began to stir in my mind, and I asked which of the workmen were skilled in building and stonework. The thought became a discussion and then a plan. By the time a sickly dawn crept over the ruined city, a band of us were already hard at work.

That night, I looked out through a crack in a shutter from a house as night fell on the pitted roadway and the ill-used buildings. Briefly, I wondered what kind of rulers poured a city's wealth into fruitless warfare while their people's homeland fell apart. Then my eyes focused on the misty street below the window. Beside and behind me, other figures waited, motionless.

A pretty fair-haired girl, not yet a maiden, strolled from the doorway to the empty road. Her pale hands worked at a piece of cloth, sewing a pattern into it. The thin light of a new moon glinted in her hair. It seemed that in all the world nothing moved but her fingers, and the stitched pattern was the story of all our lives.

Then, from the shadows behind a long-derelict temple, something emerged. It walked on two legs, but it was not human. Its flesh was grey and scarred with running water. In its long corroded face there were no eyes. Its hands were swollen fists, a single vicious talon curling from each. Even from the high window and across the street, I could smell the thing: a mass grave, an infected wound.

The girl saw it and bit her hand; the creature was too hideous for screaming. As its stumbling approach quickened, she backed through the doorway of the house where I and the others waited. The horror was still outside the door when the girl escaped through the back window; the rest of us followed her, taking up positions behind and on either side of the rotting structure. Nobody had lived in this house for a generation.

Through the previous night and day, skilled workmen had made the house a trap. The walls stood on thin struts of rock, chipped to a balanced minimum. Untouched, the house stood firm enough. But as a dozen men rushed to put their shoulders to its walls, the structure cried out. The stumbling fiend that had thought to plunder a home was caught between walls that crumbled and fell. The crash echoed through the still night.

It took us a long time to uncover the remains of the nightmare from the broken stone and wood that covered it. What we finally saw by the light of a hanging fingernail of moon was a shattered, inert mass of dead flesh that reeked of the marsh. No sane god could know how many bodies the wasteland had given up. At the still warm core of the fallen creature of ruin there lay a human figure – its back broken, its mind deranged, but still unmistakeably the sorcerer whose cold life had blighted the city and whose avatar had tormented me in the waking world. As I gazed at his insane, mocking face, the young girl who had served as a decoy first spat on it, then used a heavy fragment of stone to teach it silence.

I awoke shaking and weary to the scratching of rain at the window, only minutes before the alarm clock started another working day. As I gulped bitter coffee and dressed, it occurred to me that hope did not lie in kings and heroes but in the hands of ordinary men and women. The ruined city belonged to all of us, and so did the struggle to bring it down and build one worthy to be lived in.

But I still dream of blood and battle, still glimpse the sunset on broken walls of ancient stone. And the dreams sustain my waking days. I see a hidden life in the streets around me: in the cheapest of buildings, the most stunted of trees, the most silent of people, I see a power waiting to be unleashed and a dream waiting to be realised.

A LONG WINTER

The start of winter is always fucking miserable. A sudden chill burns up the dead leaves with fever, the naked trees are wreathed in mist, and the four horsemen of seasonal disease – influenza, bronchitis, gonorrhoea and depression – ride into town on their rachitic horses. The game is up. So for reasons we barely remember, we bookend that bitter week with festivals that dramatise the struggle of faith with its two permanent enemies: magic and heresy. The bonfires tell us that rebels will always burn. And so we're set for another winter of dull-faced obedience, with the festive season placed right in the middle to reinforce the values of work and family. It makes me restless, to be honest. And when I get restless, things start to happen.

I'm not a leader, but somehow it often kicks off when I'm around. Maybe I like to pour fuel on the flames. Late November was a case in point. I'd been out with a couple of mates, who'd run into a few more, and the mood had soured as the conversation turned to the benefits and handouts that are bleeding the economy dry. No jobs, no mortgages, but there's always cash for beggars. So as we staggered to the bus stop I kept up the theme, muttering and chanting, holding the group together, until we chanced on a cripple hiding in a doorway. I pointed the finger and my friends did the work. No serious harm, just a few teeth knocked out. Probably raised his benefit rating.

The following night was about love, not hate. Nobody could say I've got a one-track mind. More like an iPod in fact: all the classics, plus some stuff you've never heard before. I was out with Carl, one of my friends from the previous night. He liked the look of a punk girl in a nightclub, but she was a bit down for some reason I never got to the bottom of. I niced her up, used all my boyish charm, then won her trust conclusively by introducing her to my friend. In no time at all she was agreeing to go home with the two of us. It was their show. He fucked her passionately as I watched; then they slept as I lay beside them, basking in their shared warmth.

A few days later, Carl and I had a falling out. He was asking me for a shoulder to cry on, and I don't do that, I'm not a fucking Samaritan. I couldn't work out if he was more bothered about the girl or the beggar. I told him they'd both got exactly what they needed. It was all good. But he was getting wound up, started blaming me for what he'd done – so I told him that when all relevant evidence was taken into consideration, it was clear that the likelihood of it sucking itself was low. He went quiet for a bit, then started telling me his life had no meaning. I said the river was only a mile away, he knew what to do.

We walked together down the hill from the Moseley pubs to the bridge. I always love the view there, you can see clear to the city centre. To our right, the window lights of a housing estate hung suspended in the mist that smeared them into a rune. Life is full of revelations, but they're wasted on common people. We got to the bridge and Carl just stood there, his mouth working like an actor's in a silent film. Then he lost the argument and pale fluid gushed from his lips as his neck jerked in pain. I looked past him at the trickle of dull water coming from underground – a river by local standards, but not by mine. If he jumped he'd break his back, not drown, which was fine by me. But he didn't. After a while I left him to it.

Don't get the impression that I skulk around like Toffle, remembering lost friends and lovers. I'm great at making friends. It's just that they always expect too much. And to be honest, when the company gets thick and the confidences start flowing, my mood can sour a little. I remember how little there was of me before they gave me a voice. That's where the anger comes from, I guess. That and knowing what shits people really are when the masks come off. Life is a solo journey. But like Tove Jansson said, a song is better than a suitcase. And as the nights close in and the artificial fir trees glow, there are plenty of songs – and plenty of friends.

It's the few that I care about though, not the crowd. The ones I go back a long way with. They're mostly alone over the festive season, so I make a point of keeping in touch. What I share with those deeper friends is a far more important message than any cheerful evangelist nonsense. *You are special. Nobody else is worth trusting. Be true to yourself. If you have to lie to other people, it's all they deserve. Every word of theirs is a lie anyway.* They already understand, of course – their own lives have proven it to them. But you have to fight the propaganda.

Did you know that the early Church shifted X-Mas to late December so it could replace the traditional solstice festival? Didn't entirely work, of course. The weekend before the Te Deum descends (thanks to Mr Bierce for that pun) is a strange and wild time – a time for getting lost, getting pregnant, getting hurt. Not so much a pagan ritual as the shadow of one, with concrete flyovers and tower blocks replacing the standing stones. It's a reminder of where we belong, which is nowhere. I wouldn't miss it for anything. New Year's Eve is better known, but it's really just a formalised echo of the solstice. On New Year's Eve your cards are already marked, but that last night out before X-Mas belongs to the unknown. The carols can't drown the older music drifting between the unlit buildings.

This year, I got to Broad Street in time to see the sales force let off the leash. Their office maturity came apart as quickly as their office outfits. By nine o'clock, the perfectly made-up eyes were smeared and bloodshot. By ten, the flawless white shirts were half undone and stained with blood, wine and cigarette ash. The spell of the unknown was on them: they had no idea where the night would take them, or what kind of release the hands laid on them would bring. The clamour of seasonal pop records couldn't mask the insidious call of the winter song.

A beautiful young woman with cropped red hair was crying into her wineglass. Her office love affair had ended, and she had a joyless winter break to get through before trying to salvage her job. I touched her cheek and told her about the ravens of destiny whose wings were flapping over the canal. Her eyes misted with vision. Perhaps she'd end the night writhing in the arms of a new lover. Or else writhing on the floor alone, vomiting from the acid hollow of herself. I'm not a fortune-teller.

In the Gents', a young man with a bloated face was staring into a mirror. I put my hand on his arm and said gently: 'You look like shit, pal. I'm telling you for your own sake.' He wiped his mouth, shivered and said something about a jealous girlfriend. I gave it to him straight: 'Only one thing gives the modern woman pleasure, and that's cutting off a man's balls.' He was weaving as we re-entered the bar, so I steered him to the doorway. Outside, revellers were milling across the bridges between the restaurants and pubs. I picked up a bottle, neatly broke off its end and put it in his hand. One of the ravens flapping overhead settled briefly on his shoulder.

I connect well with individuals or even small groups – and I'm very good at couples – but a crowd has its own more elusive mind, white noise with no clear signal. So I was surprised, and even excited, when the revellers scattered across Broad Street that night began to draw together. Instead of leaning in shop doorways or roaming the street in search of a taxi, the young remnants began to assemble, gathering into pairs or groups, healing the open wound of the roadway. The winter song blew clear across the Grand Union Canal to the waiting multitude.

The stars flickered as if on the point of going out. It was a bitterly cold night, though you wouldn't know it from the way most of the celebrants were dressed. They moved silently through the gates to the Brindleyplace development on both sides of the canal. More and more people came, huddling together in the dim light, the crowd spreading down onto the canal-side, filling the view in three dimensions, a sleepwalking march.

From the city side of the canal, a young woman dressed in white stepped out across each of the three bridges. I wasn't sure if there were really three girls or just three images of the same one. From the other side, the factory side, a young man in a black suit walked onto each bridge. They met halfway and embraced, kissing with a hunger I could feel even at quite a few yards' distance. Then they stepped past each other, turned to face the opposite sides of the bridge, and jumped. The water rippled and was still again.

Minutes passed, but nothing rose to the surface. The crowd lost its focus, drifting and breaking up. Taxis filled the roadway and people began to disappear. There were some arguments, but no fights. Soon I was alone on the canal walkway, staring at the dull water and struggling with a combined sense of triumph and failure – like a seducer who's got inside but peaked too early. People are always a disappointment. You offer them another world, and all they want is to find a way home.

RITUALS

The factory was under a railway bridge, near the old post office in Digbeth. It had been disused for ten years or more. Beck had got the keys from one of his business contacts and dispatched his team there. It was a wretched night: heavy rain was dissolving the snow and ice of the previous week, leaving a wet grey blanket that reeked of car exhaust. There were four of them – plus Dalton, for whom it was a surprise party. They'd picked him up outside Bar Selona at midnight. He was in the back seat, wedged between Finlay and young Ross. The inside of the car smelt of aftershave and sweat. Finlay could feel their guest's tension increase as the car drove slowly through the Digbeth backstreets, past Victorian urinals and long-abandoned cars, in the weak light of the streetlamps. Nobody spoke.

Under the bridge, Colter parked the blue Metro next to a corrugated-iron wall and they got out. Ross linked arms with Dalton and Finlay walked behind them, glancing down the street as Colter unlocked the rain-blackened door. Something dark ran across the edge of the tunnel. The door swung open, releasing a sour wave of ammonia. Maxwell unzipped his black holdall, took out a small flashlight and shone it into the passage. The walls were spotted with mould, and the plaster had split. Finlay noticed a couple of footprints in the pale dust. No doubt Beck had used this place before.

When they reached the staircase, Dalton froze. Finlay punched him in the back irritably. He wanted to get home. Maxwell said: 'If we're going to play silly buggers, we can be here all night. Nobody will hear anything. I'd recommend not.' Dalton lowered his head and walked with the others up the metal stairs. Their feet stirred up flakes of rust and echoed from the hallway above them. Finlay wasn't entirely sure what Dalton had done. But what mattered was that he wouldn't do it again. Even through his boots, the building's cold was making his feet numb. But he could feel the solid weight in his jacket pocket – like a pacemaker, it gave his actions a steady rhythm that wouldn't fail.

On the landing they stopped at a double door. Colter pushed; it wasn't locked. They stepped through, and halted. An electric lamp on the floor lit up two men dressed only in leather jackets and boots. One standing with his back to a workbench. The other, a teenager, kneeling in front of him, sucking his cock. On either side of the circle of light were two men with camcorders. Around them were dust-coated machines on benches. Finlay heard the double doors swing shut.

'Fuck!' one of the cameramen said. It probably wasn't a direction. The standing performer opened his eyes and shuddered as if he'd received an electric shock. Finlay realised the intrusion had taken him to the scene's end-point. He reached in his jacket, took out the gun and said: 'Get out of here now.'

The boy rose to his feet and turned, wiping his mouth. He was dark-haired and very thin; his prick was erect. Embarrassed, Finlay looked to one side. So when the boy ran straight towards them, he was taken off balance and fired without thinking. Even as the shot echoed through the abandoned building, he was thinking: *He's just heading for the door.* The bullet tore through the boy's side and sprayed the electric lamp with blood. He fell and curled up, twitching.

The men around Finlay turned and rushed out through the doorway. He stared for a moment at the scene, then dropped the gun and ran after them. If there was any sound from the workshop, it didn't reach him. They were back in the street before it occurred to anyone that they still had business to attend to. Colter signalled to Finlay to use the gun. Finlay gestured that his hands were empty. Dalton was running away, through the tunnel to Fazeley Street and the city centre. Nobody went after him.

Three days later, Finlay was drinking in the Black Eagle when some bloke said: 'Did you hear about the shooting in Digbeth? Some benders were making a porn film in a derelict factory when a bunch of drug dealers walked in on them. They shot one of the "actors". The director was quite upset, but now he's selling the DVD for two hundred quid a copy.' The group of drinkers laughed.

'The police made a statement,' said another slurred voice. 'They're keeping the body for examination, and there'll be another bulletin later.' More laughter. Finlay wondered if the topic had been raised to test his reaction. Rumours spread fast.

Beck had refused to speak to him. The third time he'd tried to get through, an unfamiliar voice had warned him that 'Sorry' might not be good enough. He'd hoped to redeem himself by sorting out Dalton, but the problem had been found beaten to death in Walsall. Local boys never ran far enough.

Finlay raised the glass – neat vodka, his fourth or fifth – to his lips and shuddered as the cold spirit went down. The first guy was talking again: '…think they'd want to keep it quiet. But the night before the funeral, all the local queers are holding some kind of vigil in Digbeth High Street.'

He was faintly surprised that there would be a funeral. It made him think of Sean, the boy at his secondary school who'd died in the third year. Leukaemia. The roses dropped into the grave, thudding like bullets.

———————

The bedroom was cold. Finlay had got home drunk and forgotten to put the heating on before crashing out. He was lying on his side, curled up under the duvet. His cock was painfully hard. For the third night in a row he'd dreamt about the boy. Seen him kneeling on the dusty workshop floor, his lips around the barrel of a gun. Waking up as the gun fired. He glanced at the alarm clock. Half past three. What was wrong with him – was it desire or guilt? Either way, it made no sense.

Rain was scratching at the windows. As a child, he'd believed the outside world was only a city in daylight: after nightfall it became a forest, impossible to find your way through. He'd found a story called 'Finlay the Hunter' in some book of traditional folk tales in the children's library in Yardley. It was about a hunter who'd been walking through a forest all day without catching anything, and was tired and hungry. He knocked at the door of a cottage in the heart of the forest, and a very old woman answered. She invited him to come in, but said there was nothing for him to eat. As they sat in the deepening gloom, he heard wolves howling close by. 'My sons will be home for dinner soon,' she said. He reminded her that she'd said there was no food in the house. 'There is now,' she said.

As he drifted back into sleep, the boy's pale figure crouched over him. The darkness in his mouth was tearing his face apart. Finlay lay on his back, drawing cold air into his lungs. He wanted to get another drink. He wanted to cry. He wanted to masturbate. All he could do was lie still. 'Sorry,' he whispered.

———

Purchased from the corner shop, the *Sunday Mercury* comforted him with robberies and beatings until page six: a half-page story with the headline 'Seeds of a doomed life'. It speculated that the dead boy – named as Lee Winter – had been targeted by a 'gay Mafia' controlling the trade in drugs, rent boys and illegal porn. The director had apparently recruited his team from a backstreet nightclub that had no singers or disco, just dark rooms where no laws or barriers applied. There was a small photo of Lee, probably taken from a bus pass. His face was tilted, his mouth half open. There were streaks of light on his cheekbones. Finlay couldn't shake off the impression that the boy was looking past him, at something over his shoulder.

———————

Finlay shivered. The club was hardly warmer than the street outside: a concrete floor with a few barrels for seats, a bar where drinks were passed through a chain-link fence. A bowl of foil-wrapped condoms stood on a low table. Set in the wall, a huge TV screen showed two men fucking silently. It looked like a punishment. Finlay bought a glass of vodka, though he'd already had too much to drink. He should have gone home. Couldn't they tell he didn't belong here? There was a risk he might even be recognised, and what would they do then? At least his leather jacket meant he wouldn't stand out. The unlit doorway beside the bar was curtained with black crêpe paper. He stepped through it.

A dark corridor led to another doorway, another passage. He glimpsed single men waiting in alcoves. There were mirrors in the walls, but nothing for them to reflect. A side door led to a flight of stairs, but the next floor was just the same: narrow passages that looped or twisted, leading nowhere. This was the forest. Just as he was losing all sense of direction, he stumbled into a clearing: faint overhead lights revealed a web of black fabric, pillars like tree-trunks. Men were standing in pairs, holding each other. It was like a still image of a dance hall.

Finlay walked slowly through the artificial foliage. Techno music drowned all other sounds. A hand touched his arm. They exchanged glances, just enough to ensure they were strangers. The hands moved over his jacket, feeling the leather itself rather than the flesh beneath. Finlay dropped to his knees, reached up and cautiously touched the man's crotch. Fingers tightened in his hair. He closed his eyes and felt for the zip. Maybe after this, he'd be able to sleep.

As his mouth closed on the short penis, Finlay remembered the boy rising to his feet. He rocked slowly back and forth, as if praying. Rough fingers stroked his cheek. Then the rhythm broke: the man tensed and shuddered. Finlay's mouth was filled with a chalky fluid. Its scent was in his nostrils. He gagged, leaned back, swallowed. His eyes opened, but he saw only motionless trees and shadows. The man had gone.

It was raining when he left the club. There were no taxis in sight; he'd have to walk to New Street Station. The roadworks at the top of Hurst Street were covered with black tarpaulins. There was hardly anyone about. Veils of rain crumpled between the streetlamps. The unlit woman in the pane of glass above the porn cinema doorway was a shadow. He could see the rain turning to hail, but he was too drunk to feel the difference. Then he slipped and fell, jarring his knees. The wind whipped tiny hailstones into his face. He looked up, and the city's light shattered around him like a stained-glass window.

Confused, he rose to his feet and stumbled onward. The smell of vomit from a doorway made him retch. The pavement was marked with still ripples of hail. A taxi passed, the driver sounding his horn for no apparent reason. Finlay raised his finger at the disappearing vehicle. Coming back to the finite was so painful that at that moment, he could have killed just about anyone. Before he got to the taxi rank, he stooped and picked up a fistful of hailstones from the gutter. They took a while to melt, and left his hand clenched in a miser-like posture.

———————

They were waiting in the porch. Four young men, none of them known to him. Finlay went with them in the car. There was no point in resisting. Probably they weren't even aware why they were going to do it. They were just beginners, keen to belong, to uphold the rituals.

BEHIND THE CURTAIN

You know how some days transfigure you with the thrill of being alive? How the daylight seems to fill your lungs, making every sight and sound perfectly clear? How you look at the people around you with a renewed sense of compassion and even wonder, seeing the inner strength that takes them through every challenge the world throws at them? This wasn't one of those days.

It was late May, but there was frost on the ground before it even got dark. A restless wind scratched the cars with litter. The pale clouds that had bleached the view in the morning were stained with yellow as the hidden sun went down, trapping the city in a bell jar of its own light pollution. I felt almost too weak to satisfy my need, but knew if I didn't the next day would be even worse.

After hours of sitting by the gas fire, its sullen glow making my hands translucent, I put on a jacket and went out into the street. No traffic was moving. It was three o'clock. Within minutes my hands and face were numb, but I kept going. I'd surrender to the cold if that was all the city had to offer. The breath trailed from my mouth like an apology for ectoplasm. Razor wire glittered on factory walls as I walked through the Nechells industrial estate. I undid my sleeve button and touched the inside of my arm, tracing the scars with a thumb.

Crossing the bridge over the canal in Livery Street, I glanced down at a shifting light on the towpath. A group of drunks were sitting around a heap of burning rubbish. There must have been some plastic in the fire: my mind twisted suddenly, and I almost collapsed. With one hand over my mouth, I kept on through the subway and up onto the main road, just in time to see a car drive through the front window of a computer shop. The alarm tore through the night, but no one reacted except by quietly sloping off. I remembered a recent story that was doing the rounds: the ram-raiders who'd jumped back into their car to find that kids had made off with the back wheels.

The need guided me, but it was no compass. What I needed was getting harder to find all the time. They were a dying breed. Like urban foxes, they were facing too much competition and a toxic environment. Maybe, given time, they'd learn to think outside the box. But time was something none of us had much of. And if they wasted away, faded like an infection in a dead limb, where did that leave people like me? Shivering in the backstreets, wrapping our bony arms around a pain that, no matter what we did, would never hurt enough.

Out beyond Snow Hill, among disused factories and warehouses that were just finding a new lease of life through the sex industry, I felt somehow closer to what I needed. It was the confusion of stone and flesh, the smell of used condoms and cheap perfume permeating the rotten brickwork, that soaked into my body like water into dried flowers. I walked past the temporary porn cinemas and all-night massage parlours, avoiding the eyes of the painfully thin girls who waited at the bus stops. They couldn't give me what I knew I wouldn't sleep without.

At the far end of the red light district, a housing estate had been awaiting redevelopment for decades. The unlit tower blocks were boarded up, their ruined interiors screened off by placards and tarpaulins. It was a stage set under wraps, behind the curtain in a theatre whose opening night would never come. There were no streetlamps here, and soon I was walking in almost complete darkness. Years of night vision, and an obsessive sense of smell, informed the landscape for me. Where someone else would see shut-down ruins, I saw dens and burrows.

Even so, I was creeping around there for a couple of hours before I found what I was looking for. A broken window, a basement where the rotting carpet was scattered with damp soil. A smell like an open wound not quite gone bad. Moving slowly and cautiously, I slipped inside and flicked on my tiny pocket torch. At once, I saw him in the corner of the room. He was naked; his skin was a pale grey. His face was like a badly weathered gravestone on which someone had once chiselled human features. He didn't move: just stared back at me as if I were a reality TV show at its nadir of tedium.

Then his face twisted, the dry lips cracking as he tried to speak. His voice was resonant from the dead space in his lungs. I could smell rotting stone and flesh on his breath, a vaguely sexual odour that took me back to my schooldays and the changing-rooms in the old pavilion. Your first desire never leaves you. It took me a few seconds to register his words. 'Go fuck yourself with a broomstick.'

'I don't mean you any harm,' I said.

He sighed, the sound of the wind in a dead forest. 'I wish you did,' he muttered. 'It's just that... well, you won't get old enough to understand how I feel. There's no pride in this.'

'I don't want money.' His dull red eyes told me he knew that too. I unzipped my jacket. The basement was colder than the streets. 'It took me a long time to find you. That means something. I'll prove it to you.'

He laughed silently, and I saw how damaged his teeth were. At least they had edges, if not the original ones. 'I'm not putting you down. Well yes, I am, but it's not personal. There was a time I could have had anyone I wanted. And I did. Not by force. I made them volunteer, whether they intended to or not.' His dry voice trailed away. I waited, shivering. He reached out in the dark and gripped my hand. I felt his nails in my skin like brittle thorns.

'The game's up,' he said at last. 'Like the gypsies, we're dying out because there's no place for us. Our trades are gone. And those films just added insult to injury. If you can't be photographed, how can you be in a film? Not much chance of a castle when you can't rent a cunting bedsit without an ID card. You can't even participate in happy slapping. You won't see one of us on *Big Brother*.'

'Maybe the camera's the vampire,' I said.

He threw my hand back at me. 'Do I look fucking postmodern? Do I?' He breathed the reek of stale carrion onto my face. 'Don't be clever with me.'

I bit my lip. It looked like I'd have to make the running. My fingers were numb with cold, and I struggled to unbutton my sleeve. 'It's been a while,' he whispered. 'Don't have the strength. Can't even hunt rats. The one good thing this government's done is banning abortion. Means in a place like this, there's a steady supply of live snacks. Left to wail behind the tarpaulins. I should make them last, but I can't. I just bite the head off and drink from the artery.'

His withered claws tore my shirt open, scattering buttons in the black soil. 'I suppose you'll do, fanboy. Just don't expect the full Anne Rice. Would you kiss a bowl of cornflakes?' He raised my left hand towards his mouth. I sank to my knees, my right hand pressing against my crotch.

As the skin of my wrist broke, I felt two of his teeth wobble and lose their grip. His tongue flickered to catch the trickle of blood. 'Fuck,' he snarled into the palm of my hand. Crouching, he fumbled among the rags and decaying trophies that made up his bed. 'Where is it?' Then he raised something, and I heard a click. The red glare of his eyes reflected in a steel blade.

He cut my arm so hard I cried out, but didn't struggle. His teeth held the wound open, and his tongue plundered it. After a few minutes I very slowly unzipped and stroked my cock. We stayed in that position for maybe half an hour. I was close to passing out from loss of blood. Finally, he withdrew his ruined teeth from my arm. 'Go and clean yourself up,' he said with obvious distaste.

When I'd zipped up my jacket and was trying to coax some feeling back into my left arm, he reached out and touched my face with the splintered tips of his fingers. 'It's nearly dawn,' he said quietly. 'Fuck off home.'

I'm not keen on shared mornings either. But the loss of blood made me feel suddenly helpless. 'Where do I go?' I said.

His reaction wasn't the icy sarcasm I expected. Rather, he pressed himself into the corner of the room, avoiding the faint traces of daylight that were creeping through the broken window. 'It's your world,' the creature said. 'We can't haunt it any more. The death you bastards have made for yourselves is too huge and too close and too permanent. The night isn't ours, it's what you are. Enjoy. Dance in the graveyard you used to call a city. Try to find a home. Try to love and pay taxes. Get a life, if that's what you want to call it.'

I waited, but there was no farewell. The grey blur in the corner of the derelict basement looked like it had never been alive. Fighting the stiffness of my limbs, I crawled out through the window and parted the tarpaulins that hung from rusting, decades-old scaffolding. Somewhere behind the gaunt black shapes of the housing estate, a reddened sun was floating into the sky. As I walked back towards the city centre, pressing my cold left arm against my chest, thin snowflakes began to drift around me like flecks of dried blood.

Joel Lane was the author of two novels, *From Blue to Black* and *The Blue Mask*; several short story collections, *The Earth Wire*, *The Lost District*, *The Terrible Changes*, *Do Not Pass Go*, *Where Furnaces Burn*, *The Anniversary of Never* and *Scar City*; a novella, *The Witnesses Are Gone*; and four volumes of poetry, *The Edge of the Screen*, *Trouble in the Heartland*, *The Autumn Myth* and *Instinct*. He edited three anthologies of short stories, *Birmingham Noir* (with Steve Bishop), *Beneath the Ground* and *Never Again* (with Allyson Bird). He won an Eric Gregory Award, two British Fantasy Awards and a World Fantasy Award. Born in Exeter in 1963, he lived most of his life in Birmingham, where he died in 2013.

These stories first appeared in the following publications: 'Those Who Remember' in *Gutshot: Weird West Stories* (PS Publishing, 2011) edited by Conrad Williams, 'In This Blue Shade' in *Black Static* 34 (2013), 'A Faraway City' in *Where Are We Going?* (Eibonvale Press, 2012) edited by Allen Ashley, 'The Willow Pattern' in *The Ex Files* (Quartet, 1998) edited by Nicholas Royle, 'Echoland' in *Shadows Edge* (Gray Friar Press, 2013) edited by Simon Strantzas, 'This Night Last Woman' in *Birmingham Noir* (Tindal Street Press, 2002) edited by Joel Lane and Steve Bishop, 'Birds of Prey' in *Murmurations* (Two Ravens Press, 2011) edited by Nicholas Royle, 'The Last Gallery' in *Midnight Street* 12 (2009), 'Making Babies' in *The Urbanite* 8 (1997), 'Keep the Night' in *The Third Alternative* 12 (1997), 'My Voice is Dead' in *A Season in Carcosa* (Miskatonic River Press, 2012) edited by Joseph S. Pulver, Sr, 'A Hairline Crack' in *Roadworks* 11 (2001), 'The Long Shift' in *Psycho-Mania!* (Robinson, 2013) edited by Stephen Jones, 'Among the Leaves' in *Peeping Tom* 12 (1993), 'The Grief of Seagulls' in *The Touch of the Sea* (Lethe Press, 2012) edited by Steve Berman, 'By Night He Could Not See' in *Crimewave* 12 (2013), 'Feels Like Underground' (with Chris Morgan) in *The Magazine of Fantasy & Science Fiction* April 1999 (1999), 'Upon a Granite Wind' in *The Alchemy Press Book of Pulp Heroes* (Alchemy Press, 2012) edited by Mike Chinn, 'Rituals' in *Do Not Pass Go* (Nine Arches Press, 2011), 'Behind the Curtain' in *Wilde Stories 2009: The Year's Best Gay Speculative Fiction* (Lethe Press, 2009) edited by Steve Berman.

The following stories were original to this collection when it was first published in 2015: 'Internal Colonies', 'A Long Winter'.

Influx Press is an independent publisher based in London, committed to publishing innovative and challenging literature from across the UK and beyond.

Lifetime supporters: Bob West and Barbara Richards

www.influxpress.com
@Influxpress